D0974803

Dirt Road Home
Alabama Moon

DIRT
ROAD
HOME

WATT KEY

DIRT ROAD HOME

SQUARE
FISH

FARRAR STRAUS GIROUX
NEW YORK

SQUARE
FISH

An Imprint of Macmillan

Library of Congress Cataloging-in-Publication Data
Key, Watt.
    Dirt road home / Watt Key.
        p.   cm.
    Summary: At Hellenweiler, a reformatory for second-offenders,
fourteen-year-old Hal Mitchell will soon be free if he can avoid
the gang violence of his fellow inmates, but the real enemy may lie
elsewhere.
    ISBN 978-0-312-67435-9
    [1. Reformatories—Fiction.   2. Gangs—Fiction.   3. Violence—
Fiction.   4. Correctional personnel—Fiction.   5. Fathers
and sons—Fiction.   6. Alabama—Fiction.]   I. Title.

PZ7.K516Dir 2010
[Fic]—dc2

22010011319

Originally published in the United States by Farrar Straus Giroux
First Square Fish Edition: December 2011
Square Fish logo designed by Filomena Tuosto
Book designed by Jay Colvin
mackids.com

10   9   8   7   6   5   4

AR: 3.8 / LEXILE: HL540L

For Albert. A good boy.

Acknowledgments

Special thanks to my wife, Katie, for her patience and encouragement, Chip Klinkow for his "insider" perspectives, and David Klass for being a good friend to a writer. Thanks to my daughters, Adele and Mary Michael; I couldn't be prouder of my two beautiful little girls. Thank you to my parents, Craig and Albert Key, and all my siblings—Betsy, Alice, Reid, Murray, Thomas, and David—for being interested in and supportive of my writing over the years.

DIRT ROAD HOME

1

Late Sunday morning Officer Pete delivered me in chains to the Hellenweiler Boys' Home in Tuscaloosa, Alabama. I was officially "property of the state" and sentenced to live there until I was eighteen. This place would be hard time, especially since I was considered a problem case and an escape risk. But I figured I could handle it. I'd already done two years in the Pinson Boys' Home. Besides, I didn't plan on sticking around long.

There were two places a ward of the state could go after Pinson: Live Oak and Hellenweiler. Everybody talked about Live Oak like it was a vacation. Nobody talked about Hellenweiler. It was for the repeat offenders and trouble kids. I was both and I'd known for a long time that Live Oak wasn't in my future. The only reason I was three months late was because it took them that long to catch me after my escape. And the only reason they caught me was because I turned myself in to help out a friend. Now he was gone and I had to face a whole new set of friends and enemies. Except this time I was no longer the biggest, oldest boy at the home. I was a new fish.

I shuffled toward the guardhouse ahead of Officer Pete, the leg shackles restricting my steps and bruising my ankles. In the distance I heard a church bell. Sundays were supposed to be the beginning of the week, but they'd always felt like the end of it to me. All I could think about were the days ahead as dread puddled in the pit of my stomach. This time the dread was so strong it made me dizzy. I blinked my eyes and swallowed against the awful feeling. Then I took a deep breath and savored the smell of the pines and honeysuckle in the spring air. I listened to the robins calling and rustling in the hedge beside me. It would be a while before I'd sense any of these things again.

When we got to the front gate I heard a buzz and then a click as the electronic lock released and the gate slid open. Hellenweiler sat in the middle of a five-acre yard of mostly bare dirt and a few small oak trees. Beyond the ten-foot wire fence was a field where nothing was planted. I guessed it was plowed to bare dirt to give the guards a clear view of anyone trying to escape. There was almost two hundred yards of open ground before you got to the trees.

You would never hear an adult call Hellenweiler a prison. It was always referred to as a "boys' home." But to look at the one-story cinder-block compound from the outside, there was no question what the place was modeled after. I had an idea what I'd find on the inside as well, and it wouldn't be pretty. I already had the feeling that Pinson had been a preschool compared to this place. This was a high-security jailhouse to lock down eighty bad boys.

I won't tell you that I wasn't nervous. I was, but not because I was scared of how they would treat me. I'd been through bad and I could go through worse. I was worried about my attitude. I knew I had it in me to be a problem. I knew I was hardheaded, with a temper set on a hair trigger.

If I wanted to get out of there before I was eighteen, I had to play it cool. Real cool.

We passed through two more electronic gates before arriving in the receiving area. The sickening smell of disinfectant and bleach hit me like it did the first day I walked into Pinson. But I would get used to it again. I would get used to the hospital-blue walls and the rotten food and the buzzers and the snapping of wall clocks marking time in the silence. There was nothing natural about the place.

Officer Pete guided me to the counter.

"This the Mitchell kid?" the receiving guard asked.

"Yeah," Officer Pete replied. "Henry Mitchell, Jr."

The guard put some forms on the counter and Officer Pete completed them and slid them back. Then he turned to me and began removing my restraints. When he was done he tucked the chains under his arm and studied me. He was stern, but I knew there was a lot of good in him that he didn't like to show. "Keep your chin up," he finally said.

I nodded.

He stared at me a few seconds more like he wanted to say something else, but he didn't. There wasn't anything left to say. Finally he turned to the guard. "All yours," he said.

I watched Officer Pete leave until the door shut behind him. As soon as the lock clicked my new life began.

"Face forward!" the guard shouted.

I jumped to attention.

"You in my face, boy?"

I shook my head.

"You better stand back behind that red line!"

I looked at the floor and saw the red tape. I backed up until I was behind it.

"And you better get rid of that attitude before Mr. Fraley gets rid of it for you," the guard said.

"I don't have an attitude."

"I'll bet you don't," he said. "I've read your file. Mister tough guy. We'll see about that."

I didn't respond. I knew it wouldn't get me anywhere. I took a deep breath and stared at a spot on the wall just over his head.

"Strip down."

I quickly took off everything except my briefs and socks and faced him again.

"I said strip down!"

I pulled down my briefs and peeled off my socks and straightened up.

He pointed to a trash barrel against the wall. "Throw it all in there."

I scooped them off the floor and tossed the wad of them into the trash barrel.

"Put your forehead on the wall, turn around, and spread your cheeks."

I did as he said while he inspected me for contraband and scratched information on my receiving forms.

After what seemed like forever he said, "Follow the yellow line through that door to your left."

I entered cleanup, where another guard was pouring some liquid from a jug into a chemical sprayer that he set down in the center of the room. Four showerheads stuck out of the wall to my right. Against the opposite wall were four stools and the same number of electric razors hanging overhead. Another door exited the rear of the room.

"Tommy, get the fleas off this boy," the reception guard said over my shoulder as he guided me onto one of the stools. He left and I heard the door lock behind him.

It took less than a minute for the second guard to give me what the boys called an onion head. Then he made me stand up and wait while he fiddled with the sprayer in silence. He screwed the top on and began pumping it full of pressure.

"Into the shower," the guard finally said. "Do not turn it on until I tell you to. Face me, close your eyes, and cover them with your hands."

I walked under the first showerhead and covered my eyes. After a few seconds I heard the hiss of the sprayer and felt the cold insecticide mist over me. Then he told me to turn around and I felt the same sensation on my back. After the chemical had time to work, he told me to turn on the shower and scrub myself. I opened my eyes just in time to see a bar of state soap tossed at my feet.

When I was done showering the guard gave me a small towel to dry off. Then he gave me a T-shirt, boxer shorts, and shower slides. I was issued an orange jumpsuit with H.J.H. stenciled on the back and #135 on the front. The instant I was zipped up he ordered me to stand on the yellow line again.

"Walk the yellow brick road into the hall," he said. "When it stops you'll be at a set of double doors. Go through those doors and you'll be home. Keep on and you'll come to the mess room. Lunch is almost over but you might be able to pick up a bite before they run you out. After lunch a guard will take you through orientation and tell you what you need to know. Understand?"

I nodded. I was stunned and couldn't reply even if I'd wanted to. Everything was happening so fast. But I guess that's what they wanted. They didn't want you to have time to think about anything but what they told you.

I followed the yellow line out into the hall. I soon came to the large set of double steel doors. When I pushed through them fifty more feet of hall lay between me and a second set of doors. I could suddenly hear the noise of the mess room. I took a deep breath and kept moving, pushing through the second set of doors.

When I stepped into the mess room, I expected everyone to stop what they were doing and stare at the new fish. That's what they'd do at Pinson. But I noticed only a few boys glance my way over all the commotion. I walked against the wall, around to where the food trays were. When I slid my tray in front of the server, she handed my plate over the counter and watched me.

"Better be quick about it," she said.

I took the tray, set a paper cup of red juice on it, and went to look for an open seat. There were five long columns of tables. The tables on the outside of each column, the ones against the walls, were mostly full. Then the next column of tables was completely empty and only two boys sat at the middle table. One of them was a giant white kid with crew-cut hair and a cookie-dough face. He was hunched over his tray, eating slowly and keeping his eyes down. The other was a black kid with wide eyes and kinky hair. Something in the way he looked at me told me I was welcome to join them.

As I started for the middle table I saw Preston sitting with some older boys against the wall to my left. He'd come from Pinson eight months before. We'd never had much to say to each other. He was a sneaky little arson and I'd never had any respect for him and he knew it. Back then he would have been scared of me. Back then I would have called him a wuss to his face.

"Find a seat, new boy!" somebody yelled.

I didn't look to see who it was. *I can do this*, I thought. *I can do this*. But the words didn't make me feel any better.

2

I approached the big white boy sitting closest to me at the middle table. "Mind if I sit down?" I asked.

He kept eating and didn't answer me.

"You can sit with me," the black kid said. He was bigger than me. Most of them were. By now it was instinctive for me to size people up.

I kept walking and sat across from him.

"How much time I got?" I asked him.

"About two minutes."

I looked at my plate. State meat patty, some kind of boiled greens, and macaroni and cheese. I knew from Pinson that none of it would have any taste. It was food designed to keep you alive and nothing more. I started stuffing it down.

"You're new here," he said.

I kept chewing and nodded.

"You thought about who you're gonna join up with?"

I looked at him, swallowed, and chased it with red juice. "What are you talkin' about?"

"Death Row Ministers or the Hell Hounds. They say you gotta claim."

"Who says?"

"Some boy told me."

I shook my head. "I ain't into that." I picked up the meat patty with my hand and took a bite.

"I've only been here three days," he said. "Both of 'em been talkin' to me."

I didn't answer him.

"They say you don't wanna be alone around here."

"I'm just stayin' out of trouble. They can do what they want."

He was finished eating. I scooped up some macaroni and cheese and shoved it in my mouth.

"I'm Leroy," he said. "From Gadsden."

I kept chewing and looking at my plate.

"I haven't made up my mind yet," he continued. "You're gonna make enemies whether you choose sides or not."

"That's up to them."

Suddenly a buzzer went off. It was so loud you could feel it in your teeth.

"Time to go outside," he said. "I'll see you later."

I shoveled some greens into my mouth. Leroy got up and headed toward the tray return. I clamped the rest of my meat patty in my teeth, got my tray, and followed him.

A guard was waiting outside the mess room to lead me through orientation while the rest of the kids went out into the yard. He introduced himself as Mr. Pratt, head of security. He looked ex-military and wore his clothes tight and his hair crew cut. He was all business and no smile.

Mr. Pratt led me a few feet down the hall and shoved open a door to our right. "Washroom, commodes," he said. I attempted to peer inside, but the door swung shut and he was already moving ahead. A little farther and we crossed the hall and went into the bunk room. It was nearly two hundred feet long with bunks on two walls and an aisle between. All of the boys stayed in the same room, he said. Leaning against one of the beds was another guard. He was pig-faced and heavyset and sleepy-looking.

"Sergeant Guval, the floorwalker," Mr. Pratt said. The floorwalker cocked his eyes at me and took inventory.

I followed down the aisle until Mr. Pratt stopped about halfway. "Rack thirty-eight, top," he said. "You'll have your schoolbooks, clothes, and supplies put in the locker next to it. Top rack, top locker. Questions?"

I looked to my left and saw bunk #38. I shook my head. He kept walking.

"Each week you will be issued a new bar of soap and a roll of toilet paper. Lose it or use it before the week is up, that's your problem. Understand?"

"Yessir."

We came to the end of the bunk room. He pointed into another large room that had no doors. "Shower room, commodes," he said. Then we exited another door into the hall again. The building was quiet now with the boys gone. I heard the faint sound of them playing and yelling outside.

We crossed and entered the rec room. It was even bigger than the bunk room. It had pool tables and television and Ping-Pong and smelled like carpet shampoo and new paint. Once we were inside, Mr. Pratt turned to me. "You know what this is?"

"Yessir."

"Good."

He led me into the hall again. Not far ahead was a door that led outside. Before we came to the door we passed another hall to the right. At the end of this hall were black steel double doors, riveted with hex nuts like an old vault. But the guard kept walking and didn't explain them.

We went outside and I heard the noise of the boys to my left. I turned and saw them playing basketball in a dirt yard. "Play yard," he said. "When it's time to be outside, nobody goes inside. When it's time to be inside, nobody goes outside. Except on weekends. You can roam on weekends. Questions?"

"Nossir."

Directly in front of us was another building a short distance across a cement walk. Mr. Pratt pointed to it. "Classrooms," he said. "Monday through Friday, seven-thirty sharp." Then he turned to me. "Questions?"

I shook my head.

"Let's go. The superintendent wants to see you."

Mr. Fraley was a short, overweight man, bald except for a strip of hair just over his ears. He had a drooping face that pulled away all expression. The rest of his body sagged like not much got him out of his chair. One entire wall of his office was covered with bookshelves. He was standing before these bookshelves with his back to me when the guard ushered me into his office.

"Behind the line," the guard said.

I toed the red tape in the middle of the room and heard the guard shut the door behind me. I waited while Mr. Fraley pulled his finger down the spines of the books. There were no chairs in the room except the one behind his desk. The rest of the office was neat and clean, with little sunlight coming through gaps in the mostly closed blinds.

Finally he seemed to find the book he was looking for and pulled it out and walked to his desk with it. He sat and studied the cover. I saw my jacket from Pinson on his desk, the folder containing everything about me since I'd been in juve.

"Have you ever heard of William Golding?" he asked.

"Nossir."

He set the book on the desk, sat back in his chair, and looked at me for the first time. "Well, you should have. He wrote *Lord of the Flies*. It's required reading in most schools."

I didn't answer him.

"That's the core of the problem you've gotten yourself into, young man. You see, they tell me to educate the boys. To reform them. But this is just political talk to our fine citizens. Feel-good talk, if you will. In reality this place is a sort of human landfill that you hide on the outskirts of town. It's nothing more than a kennel for dogs that have no hope of being claimed. This may sound harsh, but it is simply a reality that you must learn to face. The sooner, the better."

He studied me like I would have something to say. But I didn't. For years I'd heard about this place from the boys at Pinson. I was prepared and I stood there ready to soak it up and deal with it.

"That is not to say you cannot adjust," he continued. "We have all kinds of dogs here. We have mutts and bulldogs and golden retrievers. But the reformation, the education—simply feel-good talk. What do you teach to a classroom of mutts and golden retrievers?"

14

"I don't know."

"If you try to teach them how to fetch and return a stick, the mutt will learn nothing. If you simply teach them how to come when called, the retriever will learn nothing he does not already know. And there are few teachers and only so much time. So you know what they learn?"

I shook my head.

"The dogs learn nothing. There is nothing we can do."

I didn't say anything.

"A young boy's mind wants to learn whether he desires it to or not. And since he cannot learn from us, he will learn from the other dogs. He will become something between the retriever and the bulldog. He will become a mutt. Do you plan to become a mutt?"

"I plan to stay out of trouble."

"From what I've seen of your record at Pinson, I don't think it is possible for you to learn new tricks."

"You just tell me the rules. I'll do whatever I need to do."

He studied me for a moment, then reached for a sheet of paper on his desk. "Yes, yes," he said. "So you will." He held up the document and set it down again. "This is a progress report," he said. "About to go into your jacket. You know what the first question is?"

I shook my head.

"'Has the resident instigated any violent activity?'"

"I don't wanna get in any fights," I said.

"Another problem. Not only will you not learn anything here, you will be asked to choose your friends. Choosing friends in here makes instant enemies. Refusing their friendship makes instant enemies. How will you deal with these enemies?"

"I won't."

"What will you do about the things the dogs teach you?"

"I won't listen."

Mr. Fraley shook his head doubtfully. "Very well, Henry Mitchell." He made a mark on the sheet and placed it in my jacket. "You may have visitors on Saturday between eight and two and Thursday between three and six. Canteen is every Monday morning if you want to buy anything. Money must be received by noon on Friday so that it can be posted to your deposit account. Understand?"

"Yessir."

"Then consider yourself oriented. You're dismissed," he said, waving me out with his hand.

3

After the meeting with Mr. Fraley I was escorted back to my bunk and started going through the supplies kept in my locker. An extra jumpsuit, socks and underwear, a stationery kit, toothbrush. The floorwalker stood watch at the door.

It wasn't long before another guard came in and said something to the floorwalker. The floorwalker came down the rows of beds and told me I had a visitor.

I met my lawyer, Mr. Wellington, in the visitors' room. We were the only ones there. Mr. Wellington was retired for the most part and I was his only client since he'd gotten a friend of mine out of trouble. He didn't even wear a suit, but dressed in blue jeans and boots. He set his briefcase on the table and sat across from me. It was good to see him.

"It's not as bad as you thought, is it, Hal?"

"I don't know yet. I just got here."

"Well, you do the best you can," he said.

"How long?"

"I'm still working that out with the court."

"How's Daddy doin'?"

"Not very well. But it's been two days since he's had a drink. There's a lot to be said for that."

"He goin' to those AA meetin's?"

Mr. Wellington nodded. "He's doing everything he can. Now we just need to make sure you keep it steady in here."

"I'm gonna do whatever I gotta do."

"Your father's held a job for close to three years now and that's what the court likes to see. If he stays sober and you don't get into any trouble while you're here, I might be able to get you home again."

"Okay."

"I just wanted to stop by and let you know that things were in motion. Remind you that your daddy and I are doing what we can. You're not alone in all this."

"I know."

He reached into his top shirt pocket, pulled out a piece of paper, and handed it to me. "Your daddy thought you might want this," he said.

I looked at the paper. It had my girlfriend, Carla's, address on it. How did he know I'd forgotten to get it from her? I felt my face get a little warm as I tucked it away. I stood and shook his hand. "Thanks for helpin' me and Daddy."

"You can thank me when you walk out that front gate."

I nodded.

"Stay out of trouble, Hal. That's all you've got to do."

It was time for the boys to come inside and go to the rec room. I went back to my bunk and lay down. The guard didn't say anything, so I figured it was allowed. I didn't want to be around the others unless I had to. That was just asking for trouble. I'd keep to myself as much as possible. I didn't care what anybody thought about me. I didn't need friends. I didn't want them.

That evening I stood in the supper line holding my tray. The boy in front of me had a cross-shaped scar on the back of his neck. I looked over the mess room. The boys fanned out to the right or left and filled up the outside tables. Leroy and the big kid were back in the middle at their same spots.

Somebody bumped me from behind. I turned and faced Preston.

"Watch out," he said.

At first I thought he was joking. "What's up, Preston?"

"Not the big man anymore, are you, Hal?"

Then I knew he wasn't joking. "What's got you all bowed up?" I said.

"I don't need to bow up to you."

I smirked and turned around and faced ahead.

"Don't turn around when I'm talkin' to you," he said over my shoulder.

I didn't answer him. He knocked me hard in the back and my tray went clattering to the floor. I felt my temper flare, but I set my jaw against it. I bent down and began picking everything up.

"You better get some friends quick," he said.

I stood with my tray and stepped up to the food counter.

"I'm gonna come talk to you later," he said.

"Fine, Preston," I said.

The serving woman put a plate of food on my tray and I grabbed a cup of ice water. I took my supper and turned and walked toward the middle tables. Leroy was watching me. The big kid ate and stared at his food. I walked past them both and sat alone at the end. I kept my eyes to myself and began eating.

After a few minutes Leroy got up and brought his tray to sit across from me. I didn't look at him.

"Looks like the Ministers are comin' after you," he said.

I didn't answer him.

"That's them behind me with the crosses on the back of their necks. The Hounds are on the other side. They have the scar around their wrists. They use a red-hot nail."

"I told you I don't get into that."

Leroy studied me for a moment, then took a bite of food.

I motioned with my chin toward the big kid. "What about him?"

Leroy swallowed. "They call him Caboose. They say he's on his own."

"Well, maybe I'll hang out with Caboose."

"He won't talk to you."

"That's even better," I said.

"What's your name?"

"Hal."

"They won't leave you alone until you pick a side, Hal."

"Look," I said, "I don't want any friends in here. I don't wanna owe nobody nothin'. I wanna do my time quiet and short. Why don't you go back where you came from and let me eat my food."

Leroy looked hurt. He took his tray and moved away.

4

The Hounds stayed at one end of the bunk room and the Ministers at the other. In the middle it was just Leroy and me with Caboose across the aisle. I lay on my top bunk that evening, listening to the boys talking. The floorwalker stood silently at the door, his eyes scanning the room.

I pulled out my stationery and began writing to Carla. She'd only been my girlfriend a little over a week.

I'd met her at the Laundromat back home, and then she went on a date with me to the dirt track races one night. We spent some afternoons hanging out after that. I told her about my problems and where I was going and she had seemed to understand in a way that stayed with me. But then I had to go before I got to the point where I could tell her I liked her. Which I figured was the best thing for both of us. Now I wasn't so sure.

> Dear Carla,
>
> I'm at my new school now. My lawyer came by and told me he is going to try and get me out as soon as he can. He doesn't know how long it will take. If my daddy keeps his job and does not drink and I do not get in any trouble it might all work out. I am just going to lay low in here. I have seen a few boys from my old school that I know. I hope you don't find another boyfriend before I get out. I will write again later.

There were lots of things I could have told her about being in lockup. It was a place I was sure she couldn't imagine. I called it "school" just to try and make it sound better than it was. And I didn't want her knowing any more about it than she did. I hoped maybe there'd come a time when everybody would forget it ever happened to me. A time when I was just a normal person with a life outside the fence.

I read it again and made sure my spelling wasn't too bad. Then I thought about how to sign it. I figured now wasn't the time to hold back on letting her know I liked her. I might as well overdo it.

Love,
Hal

I folded the letter and stuck it into one of the envelopes they gave us. I licked it and sealed it quick before I could change my mind. Just as I reached into my pocket for the address, a hand came out and snatched the envelope away. Preston leaned against the bunk and studied it.

"Who you writin' to?" he said.

The floorwalker didn't seem to notice us. I stared at my letter in his hand.

"Who's your girlfriend, Hal?"

I looked away and didn't say anything. I heard him opening the letter. Then I saw the envelope flutter by.

" 'Dear Carla,' " he said. "Caaarla?"

"That's right."

"Ain't that sweet . . ." He continued reading. " 'I'm at my new school now.' "

"You must have some big boys watchin' your back, Preston."

"I've earned respect, Hal. Somethin' you don't have here."

"I ain't lookin' for trouble with you, Preston. Nobody else either."

He was quiet for a moment. Then I heard the paper tearing. He set the pieces in front of me. "Jack says you're gonna be with us."

"I don't even know Jack."

"You will."

"Yeah? You tell him I'm fine like I am. I won't get in anybody's way."

"Leroy's gonna go Ministers," he said.

"Leroy can do what he wants. I don't run with Leroy."

"You go Hounds and you'll get your ass kicked."

I looked away and didn't answer him. I saw the floor-walker coming toward us. Preston backed off. "You don't wanna get on the wrong side of Jack."

"Number one twenty-six!" the floorwalker boomed. "Get back to your area."

Preston turned and walked off. I got the torn letter and pieced it back together. Then I got another sheet of paper and began copying it.

Just before lights-out an awful smell came drifting over me. If it were possible, I would have thought it was sun-ripened roadkill. It was so thick and pungent that I felt like it had settled on my skin. I looked around, but no one else seemed to notice.

"Lights out!" the floorwalker yelled.

I put the letter away and got under my blanket just before he flipped the switch. Then I lay there in the dark, careful not to breathe through my nose, and listened to the shifting and mumbling of the boys.

It wasn't long before someone came crawling beneath the bunks and stood up near me. "Paco said for me to tell you there's a spot open with the Hounds if you want it," he whispered. "If you go Ministers, he can't help you."

"Who's Paco?"

"He's the leader of the Hounds. The big Mexican guy with the slick head."

"Tell Paco I said thanks. Tell him I haven't made up my mind yet."

"You go Hounds and you don't have anything to worry about. We're the oldest and the best."

"Tell him I'll think about it."

That night I heard a lonely wail echoing through the hall behind me. It was coming from somewhere at the back of the building. Somewhere near the area with the black doors. I turned and looked down at Leroy, but it was too dark to see his face. No one moved or said anything about it, like it was a noise they were used to hearing. The wailing went on for what seemed like a half hour while I lay in the dark with my eyes open and a sick feeling in my gut. With a sound like that, I realized things at Hellenweiler were probably going to get a lot worse than I'd imagined.

5

Monday morning I ate slowly and studied the Hound table. I picked Paco out of the group. He was not the tallest of the boys, but he was built like a bull. His Mexican face was pocked and dented like rough cheese. While the rest of his gang talked and joked, he remained expressionless and alert, eating slowly and cocking his eyes about the room.

After breakfast I attended class in the separate building across the yard. Our teacher was young and soft-spoken. He kept his back to us and scribbled on the blackboard while the boys joked and passed notes. I imagined Mr. Fraley had given the same talk to our instructor about the uselessness of teaching the dogs.

I carried my lunch tray past Caboose and sat across from Leroy. He looked surprised. He set his fork down and watched me.

"Thought you'd be at the Ministers' table," I said.

"How'd you know?"

"Preston told me."

"Yeah, well, they don't have initiation until Friday."

"What do you have to do?"

"Preston won't tell me," he replied. "Said it would be a surprise."

"I'd hate to know how that hot nail feels against your skin."

Leroy rubbed the back of his neck.

"Which one's Jack?" I asked.

"He's the skinny one with the black spiked hair. Next to Preston."

I looked over Leroy's shoulder and saw the boy he was talking about. I guessed he was about sixteen. He wasn't even close to being the biggest guy at the table, but I recognized the look in his eyes right away. There'd been a kid at Pinson with the same look. A crazy, fearless look. He had eyes that darted about constantly and you never knew when he'd lose his temper on you. After he bit a cook in the leg the guards had to haul the boy at Pinson off in a straitjacket. He never came back.

"What makes you wanna go Minister?" I asked Leroy.

"They seem to want me the most."

"That oughta tell you somethin'."

"Blacks and Mexicans don't usually get along real well."

"There's blacks on both sides of this room."

"Preston says now that Jack's back, Paco's bunch is scared."

"Preston's an idiot too."

"Well, that's what he says."

I took a bite of my food and didn't answer him.

"They say Jack's got a rich daddy who has a bunch of lawyers that get him out. This is his third time to come back."

"What you gonna do when he leaves again?"

Leroy stared at me. "I don't know. I just feel like I'll be safer with them."

I looked over at Caboose. He was chewing and staring at his plate. "Do what you gotta do," I said.

We got out of our afternoon classes at two o'clock and all of the boys filed through the gate into the recess yard. It was two treeless acres of packed red clay surrounded by a ten-foot fence. It smelled of sweat and hot tar from the roof. Beyond was the plowed field and then a line of trees.

I saw Caboose walk to the far corner and back against the fence and stare at his shoes. There were basketball goals at each end of the yard. Paco and his boys gathered at one and Jack and his crew at the other. Before long there was a game going at each location.

There was one more way onto the yard. A door opened from the office area of the main building. Mr. Pratt stepped out of this door and closed it behind him. He stood against the wall of the building and folded his arms and scanned the grounds.

I crossed between the basketball courts and went to the far fence, just down from Caboose. I leaned against it and turned and watched. After a minute, Leroy walked up to me.

"Preston tell you to keep buggin' me about the Ministers' gang?" I said.

"No," he said.

I frowned at him.

Leroy continued. "He says he knew you before."

"I've seen a few guys here I knew before."

"He says you were the toughest boy at the place."

I didn't answer him. I watched a basketball roll across the yard onto the Ministers' court. A chubby Hound from

Paco's group chased after it. Before he could get to it, one of Jack's Ministers picked it up. Then the Hound and the Minister were in a face-off. I saw their mouths moving but I couldn't hear what they were saying. I glanced at Mr. Pratt just in time to see him look away.

"Somethin's about to go down," I said.

The Hound slapped the ball out of the Minister's hand and bent down to get it. The Minister kneed the boy in the stomach and the Hound collapsed, holding himself. The basketballs at Paco's end of the yard were dropped and his boys started walking across the yard. Paco stepped away from the fence and straightened up and watched. Jack waved his hand and ushered the Ministers to meet them.

"What's the guard's problem?" I asked Leroy.

"I don't know."

Mr. Pratt was watching closely now, but he made no move to interfere. The gangs were now only a few yards apart and still closing on each other.

"He gonna let 'em all go at each other?"

Leroy started to answer me, but suddenly Mr. Pratt uncrossed his arms and took a few steps forward. "Hey!" he yelled.

Now the two groups were face-to-face. Mr. Pratt began walking toward them.

"Paco's bunch doesn't look that scared to me," I said.

Leroy didn't answer me. I looked over at Caboose. He was still leaning against the fence, watching his shoes like he didn't know anything had happened. Mr. Pratt stepped between the gangs and eyeballed them back to their sides of the yard. Then he pulled out a notepad and jotted something down.

* * *

I didn't go to the rec room that evening. I lay on my bunk listening to the floorwalker tap a pencil against the wall. Sometimes I would look over at him, trying to find some sign of compassion, but his pink pig face was unreadable. He always stared at nothing and seemed to think nothing.

The boys burst through the doors at seven-thirty and both ends of the room were suddenly filled with talking and joking. I stared at the ceiling and waited for lights-out. Then that awful smell of roadkill settled over me and I flipped and pressed my face into my pillow.

"Lights out!" yelled the floorwalker.

I heard the boys leap into their bunks and go quiet. I stayed like I was, breathing through the pillow fabric. It wasn't until the wailing started again that I sat up and looked down at the dark shape that was Leroy.

"What is it?" I whispered.

"Seg," he said. "Solitary."

"Who?"

"*Quiet down there!*" the floorwalker boomed.

6

Leroy took a bite of a Baby Ruth bar during breakfast and slid it back into his pocket.

"Where'd you get that?" I asked.

"Canteen yesterday. You didn't buy anything?"

"I don't need any zoo zoos and wham whams."

"I'll give you some money if you need some."

"I told you I don't need anything."

He hung his head. "I'm just tryin' to help."

"Well, don't."

Preston came up to me during recess on Wednesday. "You made up your mind yet?"

"Yeah."

"Who?"

"Nobody."

"We're gonna leave you alone for the rest of the week. After that, you got no friends."

"I don't want friends in here."

"You have to pick," he said.

"I don't have to do a damn thing."

"I'll tell Jack you said that."

I put my hands in my pockets and looked at the ground and didn't respond.

"Wuss," he said.

I felt my temper flare. I clenched my fists inside my pockets and eyeballed the tips of his shoes. After a moment he turned and walked away.

Later that afternoon Paco's recruiter approached me again.

"You goin' Ministers?"

"Tell Paco I ain't goin' nothin'. I'm mindin' my own business right here against this fence."

"You can't do that, man."

I didn't answer him.

"You don't know how this place works. You should listen to us."

"I'm listenin' to you. I just don't want any of it."

I got my first letter during mail call that afternoon. It was from Daddy. I stuffed it into my pocket and saved it for later. I wanted his voice to be the last thing in my head when I went to sleep.

After supper I stepped into the washroom in the hall. It was smaller than the shower room, with just two urinals, two commodes, and four sinks. I splashed water on my face and took deep breaths. I heard the door open and watched in the mirror as Paco walked behind me to the urinal. Fear surged up into my throat.

Paco spoke in calm, precise English. "Going nothing, you say . . . Interesting."

"I just wanna be left alone."

Paco chuckled. "There are two places where they will come for you. The first is the yard. The second is in here.

This is where there is no guard. No floorwalker. The boys call it the confessional. If they want to hurt you bad, they will do it in here. If they want to do more than that, there is one more place. But this last place is by appointment only."

I swallowed, grabbed a paper towel, and dried my face while keeping an eye on his back. He zipped up, turned, and stepped sideways to lean against the wall. He looked at me in the mirror.

"You think you can do this, but you cannot," Paco said.

I stared at the sink.

"Jack's boys will come after you. Eventually my boys will too, but Jack's will come first. There is nothing you can do in no-man's-land to avoid it. You are just an open target. You have to choose your friends."

I didn't respond.

"With me, I don't care if you choose my side or not. I've got all the people I need and Jack knows it. But I will make it easier for you. I will decide. You see, when Jack's boys come after you, I'll have my boys step in. After that, you might as well consider yourself a pledge of our gang. You will be in debt to my boys. That is how it will work."

"I don't want your help."

"Then they will keep coming after you. They will consider you an insult. A punching bag. Both sides will."

"Why are you tellin' me this?"

"It doesn't matter why."

"Well, I don't want you steppin' in."

"Okay. You know where to find me if you change your mind."

Paco turned slowly and walked out.

When I got back to my bunk, I saw that my locker was open. I picked through it and found my soap and stationery missing. A couple of boys from the Ministers' end chuckled and I looked over at them. Preston wore a smug look on his face. I turned away, shut my locker, and crawled onto my bunk.

Dear Son,

I wrote you this letter right after you left today. I enjoyed our time fishing this morning. I wish it would have lasted longer. The clay pit is too quiet without you. Mr. Wellington says he is coming to see you later on. By the time this letter gets to you he will have already been there. Listen to him good and do what he says. I'll come see you myself at the end of the week. I never knew it could be so hard to quit the bottle. But I'm going to hang in there. You hang in there too.

Love,
Dad

P.S.—figured you wanted her address, numbskull

I lay on my bunk waiting for the floorwalker to turn off the lights. The smell pierced my nose and I coughed against it and sat up, determined to find the source. Then I saw Caboose setting his shoes under the bed. And I saw his feet, plump and pale and peeling with athlete's foot. I felt like I could see the stench rising off them like fumes off of hot asphalt. "Christ," I mumbled.

Caboose cocked his eyes at me. I lay back down and breathed through my mouth.

"I guess I'll try to get assigned to one of those other racks on Friday," Leroy said.

"Yeah," I said. "Lucky you." But my careless words to Leroy weren't at all what I felt. I didn't want him to leave.

"I'm not as brave as you, Hal. I gotta go along with it all."

"If you knew what I felt like inside, you wouldn't think I was brave."

"You really have a girlfriend?"

"I don't know. I wrote her, but I haven't gotten any letters back yet."

"I wish I had somebody to write to," he said.

"It makes a difference when you got people waitin' on you. I got a daddy that needs me. Two dogs and a truck I been workin' on that raises my neck hairs every time I get a gear."

"You can drive?"

"Daddy lives in a trailer at the edge of this clay pit where he works. He let me horse around in the truck out there. We'd mud-ride and shoot guns and hang out. Yeah, I miss the hell out of it."

"You got any other family?"

"My momma's still around, but she don't live with Daddy. She don't wanna have nothin' to do with either one of us."

"My parents are in jail for sellin' drugs. I stole a car last year."

"I guess everybody in here did somethin'."

"Preston says Jack killed a man."

"And you believe that?"

"I don't know."

"Preston's full of it. Jack didn't kill no man."

Neither of us said anything for a few minutes.

"Hal?"

"What?"

"You think if I wrote your girlfriend a letter she'd write me back?"

"You don't even know her."

"Is that stupid?"

"I guess not . . . If you want, you can . . . Somebody stole my soap and my writin' stuff."

"You can buy more at the canteen."

"I wouldn't give these people any money even if I did have some."

"You can use some of *my* stationery."

"You sure?"

Leroy nodded.

"Thanks. I wanna write my daddy."

I heard Leroy get his paper and pen from his locker. Then I heard him scratching away for a while. Finally he tossed the sealed envelope up to me and I put it away to mail in the morning.

"Lights out!" the floorwalker shouted. Then the room went dark.

7

I was standing against the fence in the play yard when Mr. Pratt came over and said I had a visitor. I told Leroy I'd see him later and started toward the visitors' room.

When I saw Daddy standing there in his dusty work clothes my throat knotted up and I almost cried. His face was bedsheet white. He was covered in beard stubble and his clothes hung off him like he'd lost ten pounds. I hugged him and he patted me on the back while I buried my face in his shoulder. I smelled the grease and oil that stained his clothes, his smell, and it made me even more homesick.

"Good to see you, son," he said.

"I didn't think you'd be here so soon," I said into his shirt.

"Yeah, well, playin' a little hooky today."

I pulled away from him, took a chair, and sat across the table. "You don't look too good," I said.

"Soberin' up ain't nothin' you wanna try. I can hardly get through the day. I got all kinds of things I do to keep my mind off it."

He reached into his pants pocket and pulled out a handful of folded pop-tops and showed them to me. "Been makin' these Jimmy Carter teeth."

He reached into his shirt pocket and pulled out a wad of wet thread. "Been chewin' on this stuff and tyin' knots with my tongue. Then I go through about five bags of Red Man a day. If all that don't work, I start cussin' out the dogs."

"Damn, Daddy."

"Yeah. I guess I've been wired to the stuff for too long. Gotta get reprogrammed."

"You got your pants cinched up like a laundry sack."

"Hell, I know. I been through worse."

"Like what?"

"Well, I ain't really. I just said that."

"I got your letter yesterday," I said. "I was gonna write you tonight."

"I imagine you've been pretty tied up gettin' used to things around here."

"This place is bad, Daddy. I'm tryin' to stay out of trouble. I'm doin' what I can."

"You just lay low. Make sure you let the guards know you ain't gonna do nothin' but time while you're here."

"The guards aren't real friendly. All the boys are ganged up on each other wantin' me to take sides."

"You don't get involved in any of that. Those boys decide to get into trouble, they're gonna take you down with 'em."

"I know."

"You're just as bad as the people you run with."

"They make it sound like there's not much way for a guy like me to stay out of it."

"You don't listen to 'em. You listen to your gut, boy. You got the right instincts. They want you to think you need protection, but gangs get revenge. All that leads to is more revenge and violence."

"You better not miss any of those AA meetin's."

"Shoot, I'm at the front door handin' out flyers. They're gonna make me president if I don't watch out."

I smiled. "You better ease up or Momma's gonna come back on you."

"Gonna give me nightmares, boy."

"She know I'm here?"

Daddy suddenly looked serious. "You think it'd matter?"

I shook my head. "No."

"You want me to tell her?"

"No. I don't guess it'd do any of us good."

"She's your momma, now. What I feel about her don't have nothin' to do with how you gotta feel."

"She never did nothin' but yell at me and you both."

"Even that didn't do any good, did it?"

"I wanted to be back with you," I said. "She knew it too."

His eyes began to tear up. He wiped them with the back of his hand.

"Fat old nag," I said.

"Easy, now. Boy, you do as I say, not as I do."

"She's the one got me into all this."

"You got yourself into it and you know it. She didn't teach you how to steal and skip out on your schoolin' and smart-mouth her like you did."

"I know."

Daddy kept staring at me.

"What? I said I know."

"Good. But all that's behind us. I'm gonna go ahead and leave you now before I start gettin' sappy. You stay here and take it like a man."

38

"Okay, Daddy."

"I'm proud of you, son."

It really got inside me when he said that. It always had, and I wished I knew of a way to tell him how much.

"I'm proud of you too, Daddy."

"What you think they'll do to me tomorrow?" Leroy asked me before lights-out.

"I don't know. Put that cross on you, at least."

"You think I'm doin' the right thing?"

"I don't know that either."

"I don't see how I have a choice. They said if I back out, they'll break my legs."

"They can't do that."

"That's what they said."

"Who said?"

"Preston."

"I told you not to listen to him."

"They said I can't be your friend anymore."

I turned over and looked down at him. "Hell, Leroy! What you want me to tell you! Why don't you stop puttin' all this on me? I ain't the one leavin'."

"I want you to tell me I'll be okay."

"I guess you will if you don't mind crosses burned into your neck."

He kept staring at me.

I lay down again. "You'll be okay," I sighed. "Now leave me alone."

8

Leroy followed me to breakfast on Friday.

"You smell me back there?" I said.

"What?"

"When do we get more soap?"

"Sunday."

We grabbed our food and walked past Caboose to take our final meal together in no-man's-land. For a few minutes neither of us said anything. I felt sorry for him.

"It can't be that bad if Preston made it through," I said.

"You know I prob'ly won't have any say in things for a while."

"You do what you gotta do over there. I'll take care of myself."

"You mail that letter to your friend?"

"Yeah, I mailed it. Maybe she'll write you back. At least one of us'll get a letter from her."

Somebody yelled at us from Jack's gang. "How you feelin', Leroy!"

They laughed. Leroy turned and raised his chin at them. He looked back over my shoulder toward Paco's gang. "Paco's lookin' at me," he said. "Why's he lookin' at me like that?"

"I don't know. How come you think I'm supposed to know everything?"

"Say goodbye to Helpless Hal for us, Leroy!" Preston yelled. The boys laughed again.

"Hey!" the guard called out. "Cool it."

I looked over at Caboose. He had his head down, ignoring it all. I went back to my breakfast.

"Don't worry about it," Leroy said.

"I ain't worried," I said. But it was a lie.

When the buzzer sounded, Leroy told me bye and I nodded to him. He went ahead of me to the tray return and then on to his classroom.

When class was out for lunch I walked into the mess room and saw that Caboose was the only person in no-man's-land. I looked at Jack's group and Leroy was sitting beside Preston, looking down and listening to him.

I ate alone, not looking at anyone. I wanted to get my food down and get back to my classroom.

Caboose and I took our places against the fence after school. He got the corner of no-man's-land and I got the middle. I looked at the ground most of the time, and occasionally at Caboose. Sometimes at Jack's gang, trying to sort Leroy from the crowd.

We had about fifteen minutes left when I saw Leroy walking toward me. He came up and stood before me without saying anything.

"What's up?" I finally said.

He didn't reply. There was something in his face that I hadn't seen since the first day. He was scared. I looked at his hands and they were shaking.

"What's wrong?" I said.

He shook his head.

"What'd they do to you?"

"I'm supposed to hit you," he said.

"What?"

"I'm supposed to hit you."

I straightened against the fence. "That's your initiation?"

He nodded.

"Hit me or kick my ass?"

"Kick your ass."

I looked over his shoulder at Preston. He watched like a smiling hyena. Jack leaned against the fence studying me, his mouth twitching in a way that made me sick. Then I realized the whole Minister gang was watching. I glanced at Caboose and he was watching. Everyone except Mr. Pratt. I turned back to Leroy and took a deep breath. "And you think you need to go through with it?"

"I won't hit you hard. Just act like it hurts."

"You better hit me hard if you wanna get that cross."

"You can fight back. They didn't say I had to win."

"I won't fight back, Leroy. Even if I did, I don't stand a chance against you. You better go on and hit me before they catch on to what you're doin'."

"You fight me!" he demanded.

I shook my head. "This is gonna be all you, man."

He drew back and hit me in the ribs. I grunted and leaned over and grabbed my side.

"Hit me!" he said.

I straightened up and looked him in the eyes. "You better do more than that," I said.

42

He punched me hard in the stomach. I doubled over and went to my knees.

"Knee him in the face!" somebody yelled.

"Hey!" I heard Mr. Pratt yell.

"Hurry up," I mumbled. "They're—"

He hit me across the face and I fell sideways. I rolled over and looked at him. Tears were coming down his face. "Kick me," I said.

He shook his head.

"Get it over with," I said.

He set his jaw and drew his leg back and kicked me in the stomach. I closed my eyes and puked on the ground and rolled over and hugged my knees to my chest. I turned my cheek to the dirt and opened my eyes again. Mr. Pratt was wrestling Leroy's hands behind his back while Leroy watched me. I heard the cheering of Jack's gang in the distance.

"I guess you made it, Leroy," I mumbled.

Another guard came and stood over me. He didn't seem very concerned. "You wanna go to the infirmary?" he asked me.

I shook my head.

"Can you get up?"

"I can in a minute . . . I just need to lay here and get my breath."

The guard walked off and stopped for a moment to write in his notepad. I glanced back at Caboose. He was staring at his feet again.

When the buzzer clawed at my ears I was still lying

there. I heard the boys rushing out of the yard. After a minute I saw Caboose's shoes pass close by my face. I stayed there until everyone was gone. Then I pulled myself up the fence and wiped my nose with the collar of my jumpsuit. It came away bloody.

I cleaned my face in the confessional before going to supper. I could hear the noise of the kids just behind the wall. I dreaded going in there. I had a sick feeling inside that wasn't from Leroy. "They can't really hurt you," I said to the mirror. But I felt nothing behind the words.

Paco walked in. I watched his reflection as he passed behind me and stepped up to the urinal. The throbbing of my face and sides overwhelmed any fear I might have had. "I haven't seen this before," he said.

I didn't answer him.

"My boys think you must have the idea that you are better than them."

"You know that's not it."

"It does not matter what I know," he said.

"I figured they do what you tell 'em to do."

"I cannot help you now when it comes to them."

"I didn't ask for your help."

Paco didn't respond.

"What'll happen to Leroy?"

"Solitary."

"What do they do to you in there?"

"Nothing. Absolutely nothing. That is what makes you crazy." Paco reached into his pocket and pulled out a broken piece of reflective plastic. "You should keep one of these with you. You can talk to people in the other cells. It helps to see another face."

"I think I'll just try to stay out of it."

Paco put the plastic back into his pocket. He zipped his jumpsuit, came and stood beside me, and began washing his hands. "It is not too late to join the Hounds. It is late, but not too late. You can trade pride for pain."

"This ain't about pride."

Paco shook his hands over the sink and turned to leave. "It should be," he said.

They jeered and yelled jokes about me during supper. I didn't look up. I became another small version of Caboose at my empty table in no-man's-land.

That evening I lay on my bunk and listened to them down the hall in the rec room. When the boys filed in to get ready for bed, I tuned out their noise and stared at the ceiling. It wasn't long before the floorwalker came in with mail call. There was nothing for me.

Eventually I smelled Caboose's feet and heard him sink onto his mattress. Finally, when the lights were cut off, I rolled over and looked down at Leroy's bed. It was empty and stripped of its linens. I sat up and looked at Caboose. He was lying with his hands behind his head.

"Caboose," I whispered.

He didn't answer me.

"Caboose."

"Shut up, Helpless!" somebody yelled.

9

I was six days in. That morning I waited until everyone had left for the mess room. Then I got up and went after them.

As I brought up the end of the line, Preston waited for me with his full food tray. He had been easy, I thought. He would do anything for them. This was the first time in his life he'd ever felt important. I'd been a bully to him at Pinson, but he'd deserved it. And I didn't regret it. But he was having his day now. He stuck his foot out in front of me. I stopped and looked down at it.

"What do you want, Preston?"

"You're nothin' in here, man. They're gonna take you down."

I looked up. "I guess Leroy's full Minister now."

"Yeah. How'd you like that?"

"I was just wonderin' how they found somebody weak enough for you to fight."

His face went beet red and I was suddenly sorry to have said it.

"You can't touch me," he said. "They'll be on you in a second."

I stepped over his foot. "I don't wanna touch you, Preston."

He moved around in front of me. "Looks like I'm the man now, doesn't it?" he said.

I rolled my eyes. "Yeah, Preston. You're the man."

"Hey," the serving lady said. "Move it, boys."

It was Saturday so we were allowed to roam. After breakfast I went back to the bunk room while the others spent their free time in the rec room or outside in the play yard.

> *Dear Carla,*
>
> *I've been here about a week now. Daddy came to see me. He looks pretty bad. He says he has stopped drinking which is what Mr. Wellington made him do so that I can go home. I've got to keep my end of the deal too which means I can't get in any kind of trouble here. One of the guys wrote you a letter that you probably got by now. If you want to write him back you can. It doesn't make a difference to me. But write to me soon if you still want to be my girlfriend. I understand if you don't. Write to me anyway.*

I thought about the signature on my last letter . . . I felt stupid about the whole thing. This time I just kept it simple.

> *Hal*

The outgoing mailbox wasn't in its place next to the entrance door, so I stuffed the letter under my pillow and lay back down.

A guard came walking up to me later that morning. "You got a visitor," he said.

I couldn't believe it when I entered the reception room

and saw Daddy with Carla. A big smile spread across my face, and it had been a while since I'd smiled. I hugged him first, keeping my eyes on her. Then I went to her and I didn't care what she thought. I squeezed her to me and she put her arms around me like she really was my girlfriend. She was like a flower in this concrete dog kennel. The softest and best-smelling thing I could imagine.

"What you got on?" I asked her.

"That perfume you like."

"Dang," I said. "I wish you hadn't've done that."

I pulled away and looked at her. She smiled and blushed.

"I wrote you two letters," I said.

"I got your first one. I figured I'd see you before I could write."

Daddy slapped me on the back and we all sat down. "How you doin', boy?" he said.

"I'm makin' it."

"Thought you might like to have your lady friend come by."

"Yeah, it's sure good to see you two."

Carla put a package on the table. "I made you somethin', Hal."

"You didn't have to go and do that, Carla."

"I wanted to. Open it."

I opened the package and she'd baked brownies. "They look good," I said.

"They're the soft kind."

"I forgot I told you I liked those."

She nodded and I could tell she was proud of it all.

"They givin' you any trouble in here?" Daddy asked me.

I hesitated. Then I shook my head. "No," I said. "Everything's fine. Just doin' my time. You heard from Mr. Wellington?"

"He called me yesterday. Said sometimes the court moves slow. Course they're all closed up today and tomorrow."

I looked at the table and nodded. "Sometimes I wish we had a whole bunch of money and could speed this thing up. I hear you can buy out of it all if you got the money."

"Son, you got one of the best lawyers in the state workin' for you. It don't get no better than that."

"Yeah. What's your daddy think about you comin' out here, Carla?"

"He said he liked you before he found out you were headed off to the juvenile center. Says he wants you to come talk to him again when you get back."

"What's that mean?"

Carla smiled at me. "Don't worry about it. He's not as strict as he looks."

"That's good. Tell him I'll come work some chores for him or somethin'."

"You look a little bruised up around the face," Daddy said.

"It ain't nothin'. I got hit by a basketball out there."

He looked at me hard.

"I did," I said. "Stop lookin' at me like that."

After a second he nodded. "Carla, sweetheart, why don't you say goodbye and wait outside while I have a word with him."

49

We stood up and I walked around the table and hugged her again. "When I get out of here," I said, "I'm comin' to your house and set things right with your daddy."

"It's not all that."

"To me it is . . . Thanks for comin'."

She kissed me on the cheek and pulled away. I watched the door close behind her, then sat back down.

"Why'd you have to go and bring her?" I said.

"I thought you'd like it."

"I did, but don't bring her around anymore. I don't like her seein' me like this. I'll just write her letters."

"Want you to know people are countin' on you."

"I know."

"You wouldn't lie to me about that basketball, would you?" he asked.

I looked down and didn't answer him.

"You got people bustin' ass to get you out of here. You remember that."

I looked at him. I felt a lump building in my throat. "I'm doin' the best I can, Daddy. I swear it."

"You better be."

"I've been good. I ain't done nothin' wrong . . . But sometimes it's hard."

"Life's hard. You're gonna deal with it."

I felt myself tearing up and I looked away and wiped my face. "I'm dealin' with it," I said.

Daddy studied me for a few seconds. Then he stood. "Okay."

I got up and went to him and we hugged again. "I'll be back soon," he said. I nodded against him.

After a second he pulled away. "Stand up straight," he said.

I wiped my face again and straightened up.

"I love you, son."

After lunch I went to the bunk room. I got the letter I hadn't mailed to Carla and tore it open. I changed it.

> *Love,*
> *Hal*

I made out another envelope, resealed the letter, and walked it over to the box of outgoing mail. The floorwalker cocked his head my way and watched me drop it in. When I faced him again his pig face stared at empty space across the room and his mouth moved slowly like he was chewing on something.

"Can I see Mr. Fraley?" I asked.

He didn't look at me. "What for?" he finally said.

"I need to make sure he knows what happened out in the yard yesterday."

"He knows what happened."

"I didn't do anything."

"He knows what happened," the floorwalker said again.

"Can I see him?"

"No."

"I wanna go by the rules. I wanna make sure I'm doin' right. Can you let me stay in durin' play period on weekdays?"

"There's no special treatment here."

"What can I do?"

He cocked his eyes at me. "You should have thought about that years ago. I did."

I stood there, waiting for him to go on. But he didn't. He looked away again. Finally, I turned and went back to my bunk.

10

The next morning it was storming outside. After breakfast I returned to my bunk and flipped through a Tarzan comic book I'd picked up off the floor. The rain kept all of the boys inside and the building was filled with their shouting and chatter. Most of the noise came from the rec room, but some of the boys lingered in the hall. A few even wandered into the bunk room but the floorwalker's heavy stare usually encouraged them to keep moving. As much as I disliked Sergeant Guval, he gave me a small sense of safety.

At one point Caboose lumbered in and creaked down on his mattress. He put his hands behind his head and stared at the bedsprings above.

"What's up?" I said, looking over the edge of my bunk.

Caboose blinked. I frowned and looked back at my comic book.

It stopped raining late that morning and I heard the back door slamming as the boys rushed out to the play yard. Caboose eventually got up and followed them. Then the building was quiet and the floorwalker stepped out and left me alone.

I slid off my bunk to use the toilet. I was nervous about someone being in the shower room, so I headed for the confessional, hoping Sergeant Guval hadn't gone far. But the hall was empty and quiet and my footsteps echoed in the corridor. When I pushed open the door to the confessional, I heard both toilets flush at the same time and the smell of cigarette smoke drifted into me. Two boys with gouges burned into their wrists leaned against the wall. Paco's boys.

Both of them were about sixteen. One Mexican and one white boy. I'd heard them called Tattoo and Dead Eye and the names fit. Tattoo had a rough carving on his cheek that looked like it was made with a paper clip and blue ink. The other had a right eye that rested dead in the socket like whatever held it up had been clipped. Only the left eye watched me. I stepped up to the urinal.

"It's just Helpless," Tattoo said.

"Where's your friend, Helpless?" Dead Eye said.

I didn't answer them. They stepped closer to me.

"I think his friend kicked his ass," Tattoo said. "I don't think he has any more friends."

"You some kind of momma's boy?" said Dead Eye. "Maybe you need to learn how to fight."

"I don't have anything against you guys," I said. "I'm just tryin' to make it like everybody else."

Tattoo got so close I could feel the warmth of his cigarette breath on my face. "We sent you an invitation to our party. Why didn't you come?"

I didn't answer him.

"You too good for us? Maybe you think you're special."

I looked away. "I'm no better than any of you."

Suddenly Tattoo slammed his hand into my throat and pressed me against the wall. I gasped for breath as he held me there. "We saved you some cake from the party, didn't we, Dead?"

Dead Eye laughed and put his foot against the door to keep it from opening. Then Tattoo punched me in the stomach with his free hand. All I could do was draw my knees up reflexively and cough.

"But we might not invite you again. Here's some more cake."

Tattoo hit me in the face.

"And some more."

He hit me again. I felt the coppery taste of blood in my mouth. Then I saw it running down his hand.

"You spit it out. Here's some more."

He hit me again. And again. And again. Until he finally let me loose and I slid down the wall and stared between my knees, drooling blood.

"But maybe Jack and his rejects will let you play. They're not real selective. Come on, Dead. Let's let him chew on that."

After I heard the confessional door shut behind them, I rolled over and felt the cold tile of the floor on my cheek.

11

I woke to water being poured over my face and stared at the tips of black shoes.

"Wake up, kid," Mr. Pratt said.

I tried to respond, but the room was spinning and I felt like I would puke. After a few seconds he leaned down and got me over his shoulder and carried me like you would a sack of dog food. I watched the scenery blur past as I jounced up and down to his gait. We went past the mess room and through the double steel doors into the administration area. Then we went left down another hall until we came to the infirmary.

Mr. Pratt dumped me onto a bed and studied me. "Who did this?" he asked.

I couldn't answer him.

"Nurse'll be here shortly," he said. Then he walked out.

I passed out again before the nurse arrived. I had dreams of being at the clay pit with Daddy, lying on my bed in the house trailer, feeling my two dogs against me and the breezes slipping through the pines and through my open window. Hearing Daddy snoring in the room next to me and feeling safe and right. I dreamt about Carla and the time I couldn't help myself and leaned over and kissed her on the tailgate of my truck. And the way I'd felt when she'd kissed me back and then later when she'd stood behind me and put her hands in the front pockets of my jeans and pulled close against me.

I woke the next day to someone shaking me. I opened my eyes and saw an older woman, shriveled and hardened beneath her nursing uniform. I heard the noise of the boys in the distance. I wanted to plug my ears. I wanted to cry.

"You've had enough sleep," she said.

I lay there while she changed the bandages on my face and made notes on a clipboard.

"I didn't do anything," I finally said to her. She nodded absently.

"I was—"

"You can tell Mr. Pratt about it shortly."

She hung the clipboard on the wall beside my bed and left. I reached up for it and pulled it down. I read the report.

Administration Section
Resident: Henry Mitchell #135
Summary: Patient involved in violent incident
with unknown assailants.
Location: Washroom North
Comments:

Medical
Diagnosis: Abdominal bruising. Bruises around
the neck. Various cuts and bruising about the
face. Possible concussion.
Treatment: Disinfect and clean wounds,
Ibuprofen

I assumed Mr. Pratt had filled out what I saw in the administration section. The handwriting didn't match the nurse's below.

I put the clipboard back on the wall. After a short while the nurse returned with breakfast. I was eating in bed when Mr. Pratt walked in. The building was quiet and I figured the rest of the boys were already in their classrooms.

"What happened?" he said.

"They jumped me. I was just goin' about my business."

He took out his pad and a pen. "Who was it?"

I didn't answer him. After a second he looked back at me. "Don't get on the wrong side of me."

"I can't say who it was."

"Can't or won't?"

"They jumped me."

He shook his head, made some notes, and put the pen and pad back into his shirt pocket. "Okay, kid. You wanna learn the hard way, that's fine with me. I get paid the same. Maybe next time you'll be a little more observant."

He turned back to the nurse. "Go ahead and send him back out there, Mrs. Phillips."

I went to the bunk room to get my books for class. A new bar of soap, fresh towels, and toilet paper had been placed in my locker. I shoved the soap back behind the towels, hoping no one would take it this time.

On my way to my classroom I saw Mr. Pratt leading a new boy through orientation. A white kid maybe a year older than me. He looked stunned and scared. We locked eyes for a moment and then I looked away. I passed the hall to solitary and glanced at the black doors. They were closed as usual and no sounds were coming from behind them.

The instructor didn't stop talking when I entered the classroom and went to my desk. The boys watched me, but I didn't pay attention to them. I sat down and pulled my books out and stared blankly at the chalkboard and fingered the bandages on my face.

12

I was one of the first into the mess room for lunch. I got my food and went to my seat in no-man's-land. Caboose came in after me and took his seat. After a while Leroy came through the door. He was pale and weak-looking from his stay in solitary. He glanced at me and then moved on. I studied the red, crusty wound etched into his neck.

After lunch we returned to our classes. I sat through another useless lesson as the boys talked and joked and wadded-up paper flew by my face. A couple of times they tossed things at the instructor. He kept scratching on the blackboard and mumbling to himself like we didn't exist.

It started raining that afternoon, so we went back into the main building after class. I went to my bunk while the others went to the rec room. I saw that the bed below me was made up with new sheets and stocked with the usual supplies. I guessed this was for the new boy.

I heard someone coming and looked up to see Paco. The floorwalker cocked his eyes our way and shifted slightly. Paco strolled up to my bed and stopped. He began feeling the new sheets below me between his thumb and forefinger. Then he spoke quietly without looking at me.

"Now, there is only one way to avoid this," Paco said, as if he'd been thinking long and hard about my situation.

"Is this some kind of game to you?" I said.

He didn't answer my question. "I think you must become the leader yourself," he said. "You see, the leader does not have to fight. He lets others do his fighting for him."

"You had to fight at some point."

He nodded. "Yes," he said. "But just once."

"You want me to fight you?"

He chuckled. "No. That would be bad advice."

"You want me to fight Jack?"

"You see, I am a bulldog. Jack is a terrier. A bulldog rules through strength. A terrier rules with fear. They yap and bark and leap in your face. I would bet on strength any day."

"I guess Mr. Fraley gives everybody the same speech."

"He is just on the other side of a truth."

"That would be fun for you to watch, wouldn't it? Why don't you just kick Jack's ass your own self?"

"Because I don't have to."

"You've got me wrong, Paco."

He looked at me. "Tell me why it is that a person would not accept the help of others in here."

"Because I'd owe you. And I've seen what the payback is. And I promised somebody I wouldn't get in trouble here."

"You must really have a debt to this person."

"I do. It's my daddy."

"Ah, so you have some hope. You think you will be rescued?"

"He's doin' his part. I'm doin' mine."

"Yes, but can you do your part with the guards against you? They will write what they want in their notepads."

"How do you know they're against me?"

"They are against all of us."

"I don't see how fightin' Jack's gonna solve anything. I think I'll take my chances on the fence."

Paco nodded and stepped away from the bunk. He let his fingers slip from the sheet. "There is a new boy here today. Have you seen him?"

I nodded.

"As long as you stand in no-man's-land, the new boy will fight you. Each new boy. From my side, from Jack's side. One after the other. That's the way it is."

"Except for Caboose."

"That's right. Except for Caboose."

He was silent for a moment. Finally he said, "I imagine Jack will make you another offer before the end of the week."

Fifteen minutes after Paco left, the new boy came into the room. He came up to our bunk and held out his hand. "I'm Chase," he said.

"Don't waste your time, Chase. We'd both be makin' it harder on ourselves."

He drew his hand back and looked confused.

"You see Mr. Fraley?"

He nodded.

"You have any idea what he was talkin' about?"

Chase shook his head.

"Well, you will soon enough. And I'm gonna help you out some since you're just standin' there. You're gonna have a decision to make in the next couple of days. You better go Hell Hounds."

"Why?"

"Choose Hound. That's all you need to know."

"What's Hound?"

"Paco's boys are Hounds."

"What about you?"

"You'll find out about me."

He studied me curiously.

"You remember how to get to the rec room?"

He nodded.

"Go on. They're waitin' for you out there."

"Okay," he said suspiciously. "I'll see you around."

"Yeah, you will," I said.

13

Chase sat across from me during supper. "They asked me," he said.

I kept chewing and didn't look at him.

"Both sides," he said.

I swallowed. "Don't let it go to your head."

"They say you have to claim."

"Yeah, they do."

He looked at Caboose. Caboose studied his tray and chewed. "What about him?" Chase said.

"Don't worry about him."

"What about you?"

"You need to worry about yourself."

"What are you gonna do?"

I stopped eating. I stared at him. He watched me with a dumb expression on his face. Finally I picked up my tray and moved away.

I lay alone on my bunk that evening and listened to the commotion of the boys in the rec room. The floorwalker was at the end of the corridor, staring at nothing, occasionally working his jaw like a cow chewing grass.

Paco walked through the door at the other end of the bunk room. He stopped in the aisle at the foot of my bed and spoke softly to the floor. "Thank you for the referral," he said.

"I didn't do you any favors."

"He is weak, but maybe my boys will make something of him."

I didn't respond.

"You know, we have initiation on Thursdays."

"I can't wait."

"I don't make the rules anymore. I am just a spectator."

I didn't answer him.

"I think you are already a Hound."

"Yeah, you think wrong, Paco. I'm gettin' sick of this, but I ain't done with it. Maybe I'm just tired of layin' down in front of that Preston loser. He's about the biggest wuss there is. I'm gonna send 'em all your way as long as he's around. I'm gonna see him outside this fence one day and I'm gonna tear his ass up. Right up. And spit on it."

Paco smiled. "You should watch out, Hal. With thoughts like that, you may not be able to keep your word to your father."

I looked away.

"And you would disappoint me," he added.

Chase spoke my name in the darkness.

"No talkin' after lights-out," I said.

"I told the Hounds I would join."

"I know, Chase. Go to sleep."

After class on Tuesday Preston approached me from across the yard. I looked at Mr. Pratt and he turned away.

"Jack says he'll give you one more chance," he said.

"Why don't you tell Jack to come talk to me."

"He doesn't talk to nonmembers."

"Well, tell him to send over somebody I trust."

Preston's face turned red. "This is his last offer. I'll make sure of that."

"Do what you gotta do."

Preston stomped off. I watched him approach Jack and spurt out his complaint. Jack turned and looked at me. He put his hand through his hair. Then he said something and Preston shook his head and walked away.

I looked at Caboose. He was scratching lines in the dirt with the toe of his shoe.

"Caboose," I said.

His toe stopped moving.

"What gives in this place?"

His toe started moving again.

Thursday. The basketball came rolling up to my feet and stopped. Mr. Pratt turned his back.

Chase came across the yard and stood before me. "You wanna hand me that ball?" he said.

The Hounds and Ministers watched. Jack seemed to take a special interest and moved out in front of his gang.

"You're gonna have to do it without the ball," I said.

"What?"

"Go ahead. They're all watchin' you."

"You know what this is about?"

"Mr. Pratt's not gonna stay turned around forever, Chase. You better throw a punch."

"In the face?"

"You ever been in a fight before?"

Chase shook his head. I spit and turned to Caboose. "Christ, man. Can you believe this, Caboose?"

He stared at his shoes and didn't respond.

"I'm gonna have to teach this guy how to kick my ass."

I turned back to Chase. "Listen, as long as I've got a say in this, why don't you just hit me in the shoulder and I'll go down. Then you can kick me in the stomach a few times. My face hurts pretty bad from last week."

Chase nodded. "Okay. You wanna turn sideways or anything?"

"Fine," I said. "Just come on and do it."

He took a step toward me and drew his arm back. I turned sideways and held my breath and closed my eyes so I wouldn't flinch. I waited. Nothing happened. "Come on, Chase," I said.

Still nothing happened.

"Chase . . ."

Still nothing.

"I'll count to five for you. On five, you hit me. How's that?"

No answer.

"One . . . Two . . . Three . . . Four . . ."

"Don't do it," someone said.

I opened my eyes. Jack was only a few feet away and Chase had paused with his hand in the air.

Jack covered the rest of the distance to Chase, grabbed his arm, and pulled it down, watching me the whole time. "You owe me," he said.

I gazed around the yard. Both gangs and Mr. Pratt were watching us. Jack let go of the arm and it fell to Chase's side. "I won't do this again," he added.

"I didn't ask for it in the first place," I said.

"What do I do?" Chase asked me.

"You might as well go stand next to him in no-man's-land," Jack said.

"I don't owe you anything," I said to Jack. "I never will."

Jack's jaw tightened and his mouth started twitching and I saw the temper boiling up into his cheeks. "I'm gonna tell you to do somethin' right now, smart-ass. And you better do it 'cause I'm gettin' fed up with you."

I felt weak in the knees. I kept my eyes on him but didn't answer.

"Hit Chase in the face," he said. "Initiate yourself."

Out of the corner of my eye I saw Chase look at me in alarm. I didn't move.

"Hit him!" Jack yelled.

I slowly shook my head. I saw Mr. Pratt walking toward us. *Come on*, I thought to myself. *Get over here.*

Jack grabbed Chase and shoved him hard into me. Both of us fell back against the fence. "Hit him!"

"Hey!" Mr. Pratt yelled across the yard.

I straightened up and Chase rolled away and backed against the fence beside me. Jack's hand shot out and grabbed me by the throat and pinned me to the wire. He was breathing heavy through his nose, and his eyes danced with craziness.

Anger rose inside me. I clenched my teeth and balled my fists at my sides. "You can do what you want," I said. "I wouldn't join your bunch if my life depended on it."

Jack stepped closer and got nose to nose with me until his breath fanned my face.

"Maybe it does depend on it," he said.

"I didn't do anything," Chase whimpered.

"Shut up, Chase," I said.

Mr. Pratt came up behind Jack and grabbed his shoulder. Jack jerked away and kept his eyes on me.

"Back off," the guard said to him.

Jack dropped me and turned. He eyeballed Mr. Pratt until the guard looked away. "You know better than to touch me," Jack said.

"Go on back over there," Mr. Pratt said.

Jack watched him for a second more, then turned to me. "That was it," he said to me. "You just burned through your last chance."

14

That evening I got a letter from Carla. I opened it and found another envelope inside with Leroy's name on it.

> *Dear Hal,*
>
> *I'm glad I got to see you last weekend, even though we didn't get much time to talk. I hope I didn't get you too worried about my dad and what he thinks about you. He liked you when he first met you so I told him that you going away to your new school shouldn't change anything.*
>
> *I didn't tell you this, but you were my first real date. I never had a boy just come up and ask me like you did. Boys ask my older sister out all the time, but not me. Daddy says I'm not old enough, but I guess I am now! Everything will be fine, I'm sure about it. I hope you get to come home soon. I'll be thinking about you.*
>
> *Love,*
> *Carla*

I read the letter twice, then folded it and stored it under my pillow. Then the dread of where I was came rushing over me again and the smile left my face. I looked at Leroy's letter and shoved it under my pillow too. I slipped off the bunk and took a deep breath and headed for the confessional. Out in the hall I saw Paco leaning against the wall near the rec room. He cocked his eyes at me, then looked away.

I went into the confessional and began taking the bandages off my face and tossing them in the wastebasket. After a minute Paco strolled in.

"How can it be," I said, "that my only friend in here sends people to kick my ass? There's just somethin' wrong with that."

"You think I am your friend?"

"In a weird way, I think you are."

Paco laughed. "If it were true, I doubt I could admit it. Unless you joined my boys, that is."

"I haven't decided that yet."

"And I don't know that there is a standing invitation for you to join."

I didn't answer him.

"And maybe I don't invite you out of respect."

"Respect for what?"

"For a quality I have not seen in a very long time."

"What do you want, Paco?"

He paused. "There's something you should know, Hal. You must not underestimate Jack. He can be very unpredictable when you make him angry."

"No kiddin'?"

"Like most terriers, he makes a lot of noise, but he can and will try to hurt you bad enough to cripple you. That is his way. It is not tactical to him. It is not a game. It is revenge. He is a desperate coward with a mind like a nest of angry hornets."

"He doesn't seem too afraid to me."

"It is how you handle fear that determines your cowardice. He is crazy afraid. That is what makes him dangerous."

"He gonna try and break my arms or somethin'?"

"There is no limit to what he will try. You damaged his pride by refusing his gang and standing up to him on the yard. You made him look bad in front of the boys. Before, you could have surprised him. Now, he will be ready for you. You are the only thing on his mind."

"And I don't guess you'll be around to help me out, will you, friend?"

"It is not that simple. You see, for me to get involved would betray the confidence of my boys. What would they think about me helping this person who has rejected us? What would that show me to be? Perhaps I could send my boys to help you, but then I would get questioned. Why should they do this? Because I like you? That could never be."

"Well then, I guess you have some Paco words of wisdom for me?"

"No, I have a present for you. I put it in your stationery kit."

After lights-out I pulled the shiv from the stationery kit and studied it. It was like a crude ice pick. Nothing more than an eight-inch length of straightened bedspring with masking tape wrapped on one end for a handle. Suddenly fear gripped me and I shoved it under my mattress. Then

I heard Caboose's bed creak. I looked at him. He was sitting up, watching me across the pathway.

"What?" I said.

For a moment he didn't move. Then he lay back down and no-man's-land was silent.

I left the shiv in the stationery kit the next morning. I wanted it gone, but didn't want to risk carrying it far enough to throw it away.

After getting my breakfast tray, I headed for no-man's-land and looked about the room. Preston was watching me with his stupid grin. As soon as I made eye contact with Jack, he turned away and began talking to the boy next to him. I looked to the other side of the room. Paco sat amid his boys, eating slowly and silently while the others talked loudly among themselves. He turned his eyes up at me without lifting his head and kept them on me just long enough to let me know he was more alert than he appeared. Then I realized that I had not seen Chase. Even though I didn't know what became of a person that failed his initiation, I had assumed he went back to no-man's-land.

I set my tray down at my usual place. Before I could sit, somebody yelled from the Ministers' table, "Siddown, Helpless!"

For some reason, this time those words strummed a nerve in me. I remained standing, staring at my tray and concentrating on being calm.

"I think he's gonna cry!" came Preston's voice.

Anger flared and rose inside me. I backed away from the table and started walking. *This is stupid*, I said to myself. *Let it go.* But I couldn't this time. I went down to the

73

end of no-man's-land, turned, passed the dividing row of empty tables, and turned again at the Ministers' row. If the room hadn't gone dead quiet, then my ears were ringing over the noise of it. I began to pass behind them and they shifted in their chairs and swung their heads to watch me. Jack was on the opposite side of the table. When I was across from him I stopped. Leroy was directly below me. Keeping my eyes on Jack, I reached in my pocket and pulled out the letter. I put it on Leroy's tray. "Here's a letter from my girlfriend, Leroy."

I stared at Jack a few moments longer. I watched the fire burn deep in his eyes. I saw his cheeks twitching. Leroy fumbled the letter from the tray and pulled it into his lap.

I turned and continued up the table and back to no-man's-land. When I passed Caboose, he scooted his chair up.

During class that morning a note was passed to me. I looked at the boy that handed it off and he stared at me blankly. I opened it.

Boiler Room. Saturday after supper.

I sat next to Caboose during lunch. "I need to talk to you," I said to the side of his face.

He chewed slowly.

"Just tell me what the boiler room is?"

I thought I saw his mouth stop chewing for just a second, but then it resumed eating.

"I got a note that said be there after supper on Saturday. What does that mean?"

He set his fork down and swallowed. For a moment I thought he was about to say something, but then he stood, picked up his tray, and walked toward the return window.

I looked up at Paco. He was talking to someone.

"Helpless, Hal!" somebody from Jack's group yelled behind me.

"Maybe we get to him first, amigo!" Tattoo yelled back.

"Maybe we get our boys initiated!" Preston shouted across the room.

Then I saw Tattoo sidearm a dinner roll across the room. I spun just in time to see it hit the face of the boy sitting beside Preston. Jack leaped up and pointed at the guy. "Do it again, you dumb spic!"

"Bring it on, cracker!"

"Hey!" the guard yelled.

Jack glared at the guard. "Why don't you do your job and handle that!"

The guard shook his head and didn't respond. Jack sat down again and glared at me. Boiler room, he mouthed.

15

I waited in the confessional after supper. I heard the others down the hall in the rec room. It was twenty minutes before Paco casually walked in.

"What did you think of my gift?" he said.

"What took you so long?"

He stepped up to the sink and began washing his hands. He glanced at me in the mirror. "I didn't know we had a meeting."

"I figured this was part of your game. You know, havin' these little talks."

He smiled and flicked his hands dry. He ran his palm over his slick head and turned to me. "Wedge your foot against the door," he said.

"Why?"

"Because I'll leave if you don't."

I was nervous about it, but I did as he said. When I turned back around, he was sitting on the sink. "I'm not supposed to talk to nonmembers," he said. "This is getting dangerous for me."

"Welcome to the club. Why'd you give me that ice pick thing?"

"Because you are going to need it. You will need the edge, no pun intended."

"Are you crazy? I'm not stabbin' anybody! What the

hell is this place? Boys aren't supposed to be stabbin' each other in a juvenile home!"

Paco shrugged. "It is what it is."

"Christ! What the hell's the boiler room?"

"I told you there was one more place. And now you have an invitation. You will be able to fight there without the guards interfering. It is underneath the kitchen. I would show you where, but I can't be seen with you."

"Fight who? Jack?"

"Of course."

"Does everybody stand around and watch or somethin'?"

"No, it will just be the two of you. One of you will come back up and one of you won't."

I felt cold sweat on my face. "I don't wanna do this, Paco. Man, you gotta help me."

Someone tried to come in and Paco's eyes darted to the door hitting against my foot. After a second they kicked it loudly and a boy shouted, "Hey! Open up!"

Paco motioned with his chin for me to step aside and I did. He slid off the sink and calmly pulled the door to him, placing me out of sight as it swung open. He stood there facing the boy. He didn't say a word.

"Sorry, Paco," I heard.

Paco closed the door again and pointed my foot back into position. He walked over to the urinal and I heard him unzip.

"You gotta do somethin', man," I said again. "I can't get into this."

"I already did something for you. I gave you what

you need to come back up the stairs. Then you are done. You see how simple?"

"Then I'm screwed! What are you talkin' about! You think I can kill somebody and get away with it?"

"That's not what I'm suggesting. Just stick him a few times. Someone like Jack, he won't be able to stand the sight of his own blood. He'll curl up and whimper like a baby."

"Leroy said he killed a man."

"And you believe that?"

"No."

"Good. Then we can move on."

"This is crazy, Paco. I gotta talk to Mr. Fraley about this."

He zipped up and turned to me again. "About what?"

"About the fight."

"There hasn't been a fight. Besides, you have the shiv."

"Maybe I just don't go. I won't go."

"Yes, you will. So far, the boys have just been nipping at you. They are not so sure about you. They call you Help-less. They call you a coward. This is just noise. But you see, it is only their uncertainty that keeps them at bay. If you fail to show tomorrow evening, there will be no more uncertainty. And they will come in for the kill."

"What happened to Chase?"

"Chase accepted a service he could not pay for. He is gone."

"What do you mean, gone?"

"He was taken away in an ambulance last night."

I watched him, stunned. "Why are you doin' this, Paco? Why are you here?"

"Think about it. You must learn to think about these angles people take."

"I'm tired of thinkin' about everything you say like it's some big puzzle. Just tell me."

"Do you think I am your friend?"

"I don't know. Maybe."

"Are you scared of me?"

"You make me real nervous."

"That's understandable."

"Paco, you gotta stop goin' in circles on me. I need to get some help here. I don't need this boiler room stuff."

"Stay with me, Hal. What happens if you walk up from that boiler room?"

"I guess it means that somehow I kicked his ass. Then I guess I go to solitary for a while. If I take your advice and use a shiv on him, then I guess I go to the state pen or somethin'."

"I can guarantee that none of the boys will snitch. They know better. Whatever happens down there will stay down there. But that is a minor point. You need to look at the big picture, Hal."

"What?"

"You will be the leader of the Ministers."

Suddenly it all made sense. "And I wouldn't want to challenge you or any of the Hounds," I said. "And you would really be in charge of the whole yard."

He smiled. "Let's leave me out of this. Imagine for a moment that I am actually trying to help you. I don't believe that you can keep your word to your father because, as I've said, you have no control over what the guards put in your conduct report. But you can arrange things so that your stay here is more pleasant."

I didn't answer him.

"Think about it," he said.

I thought about it in my bunk, long into the night. It seemed like an impossible situation. If I didn't go down to the boiler room, they would continue to fight me. The Ministers and the Hounds would use me like a punching bag, and I didn't know if my temper or my health could hold out that long. I couldn't go to Mr. Fraley, and the floorwalker said they wouldn't take me out of general population.

I had to show for the fight. And my only chance against Jack was with the shiv. Unless I just let him beat me to a pulp. Unless he had a shiv too. Either way, I'd end up like Chase.

"Caboose?"

No answer.

"Caboose?"

"Quiet down there!" the floorwalker boomed.

16

Saturday. They left me alone during breakfast. It seemed the dining hall was quieter than usual. After the buzzer sounded I returned my tray, walked out into the hall, and leaned against the wall while the boys passed me like I wasn't there.

"You've got a visitor," a guard said to me.

There were a couple of other boys talking to their relatives when I walked into the room. I could tell by Daddy's sallow face that he was still on the wagon. He smiled to me as I crossed the floor, and I managed my own smile at the edge of my mouth. He hugged me and beat his rough palm on my back a couple of times while I rested my chin on his shoulder and closed my eyes.

We sat across from each other at a table off in the corner and I locked my hands together and studied my fingers.

"Come on now," he said. "You can't feel as bad as I do."

I looked up at him. "I'm all right," I said. "You didn't bring Carla this time?"

"You told me not to."

"I know."

"What happened to your face?"

I looked down and shook my head.

"Don't tell me another basketball hit you."

"I'm in trouble, Daddy," I mumbled.

"What'd you do?"

"I tried to stay out of it. I don't know what to do."

"We'll work it out, son. Tell me what happened."

I shook my head.

"You can't quit on me now."

I looked up. "All I've tried to do is stay out of fights. But you can't get respect in here unless you fight. And if you don't get respect, they come after you."

"You need to tell the staff. Tell 'em what's goin' on."

"They won't listen to me."

Daddy pushed away from the table and stood. "I'll talk to the boss. Where is he?"

"Sit down, Daddy. You can't talk to him. He don't give a damn about me and he don't give a damn about you."

"Where's his office?"

"Come on. This place ain't about fair. The guards turn their backs on us. You're just gonna make things worse for me."

Daddy looked around the room like he might get some answers. Then he took a deep breath and sat down again. "I feel so dad-gum helpless."

"Listen," I said. "I gotta work it out. I just want you to know that I tried hard if anything happens to me."

"Anything happens to you I'm gonna start whippin' some ass around here. Wait'll they see what a log chain and a grub hoe have to say. I'll—"

"You ain't doin' none of that. You need to drive over to Mr. Wellington's place and tell him hurry up with things."

"I been goin' up to the Laundromat and callin' him every day. He's doin' all he can."

"Go see him. He's gotta do more."

"All right," he said. "I will."

I pushed back from the table and stood. "I gotta go."

"Why you gotta go?"

"I need to think. And I don't like you seein' me like this. Maybe you can bring Carla by next weekend."

Daddy nodded to me. I didn't want to hug him this time. I was too ashamed of myself. I turned and walked away.

When I stepped onto the yard, no one paid attention to me. I crossed the dusty ground and leaned against the fence without even looking at Caboose. I took a deep breath and slid down the wire and rested my forehead on my knees. I tried to think but I couldn't.

Before supper I stuck the shiv in my sock and walked to the dining hall in a daze. I got my tray and let the serving woman put food onto it and went to my seat. The noise of the boys' normal chatter ran together and pressed into my ears like a sound underwater. I sat and bent over my tray but left my hands on either side of it. I didn't feel like eating.

When the buzzer went off I returned my tray and stepped out into the hall and stopped. The boys in front of me continued toward the rec room and the ones behind me began to pass.

"Follow me," I heard Preston say.

I fell in behind him. He turned into the confessional where Paco and I usually met. I followed and the door shut behind us. There was another boy at the sink. He had a scar around his wrist. He finished washing his hands and looked at us and left without speaking. Then we were alone.

"I'm gonna show you how to get down there," Preston said. "Jack will come five minutes later."

I nodded. Preston smiled at me.

"One of these days, Preston," I said.

"Yeah, you wish."

"You think you got friends in here? I try to get to the end of how stupid you are, but I just can't make it that far."

Preston began to flush with irritation. "You're the one that's stupid, Hal! You asked for all of this. I told you what to do when you got here, but you think you're tougher than everybody else."

"What are we waitin' on, Preston?"

"We have to make sure the hall is empty."

"You think there's enough time for me to bloody you up a little? I mean, what have I got to lose now, right?"

Preston took a step back and his hands began to tremble. "That's against the rules," he said. "This is Jack's fight."

"That's right. I'm sorry. I wouldn't want to come between you and your friend Jack. I'll bet one day when you two are out of here he's gonna invite you over to his house for dinner just about every night. Heck, I bet he names his first child after you."

Preston didn't answer. He stepped wide around me and peered out the door. After a moment he motioned for me to follow.

We continued down the hall toward the rec room, where I heard the normal commotion of the boys playing pool and watching television. We hadn't gone far when

Preston stopped before the door to a maintenance closet. He took a key from his pocket and unlocked the door and motioned for me to go inside. I stepped past him and he shut the door behind us and locked it and turned on the light. I could see that the room was really not a closet at all, but a long, narrow passageway lined with shelves of supplies. It must have gone back at least fifty feet.

"Turn around and put your arms in the air," Preston said.

I faced him. "Like hell."

"I've gotta pat you down."

"You touch me and I'll knock your teeth out."

Preston didn't say anything for a moment. Finally he said, "You don't have any weapons on you, do you?"

"Where would I get a weapon?"

He studied me. "Okay," he finally said. "Start walkin'."

I turned and started toward the back of the room. When we reached the wall there was another passageway that opened to my right. The ceiling was lined with water pipes and electrical conduit.

"Keep goin'," Preston said.

I kept on through the narrow passage for another fifty feet until I came to cement stairs. At the bottom of the stairs was darkness that flickered a pale blue like heat lightning. In its depths machinery hissed and groaned. The boiler room. I started down.

Preston told me there would be a light switch on the wall at the bottom. At the base of the stairs I faced the flickering light and felt my shoes slap into a puddle. The sweet smell of damp rust and propane fell over me. I found the light switch and flipped it on, and the boiler room was before me. It was a giant, wet basement that must have extended under most of Hellenweiler. Pipes and wires covered most of the low ceiling. Steel columns were spaced throughout the room, supporting the ceiling. Giant hot water heaters sat against one wall, rusty and fired with blue gas flames that caused the room to flicker. Several other machines groaned and clanked at the far end of the room where the light didn't reach. Suddenly the fear I'd been holding back seeped into my gut and I felt sick.

I took a few steps, faced Preston, and drew a deep breath. I knew I probably looked scared but I didn't have it in me to look any other way.

"No turnin' back now," he said.

"I guess not. Let's get this over with."

Preston turned and started back up the stairs.

17

For a minute I just stared at the cement steps leading out of the boiler room. My mind was blank and the sounds of the machinery had turned to a steady thrumming in my ears. Then I took another deep breath through my nose and turned and studied the room. I walked about fifteen feet farther and looked for anything that might help me, but it was all a tangle of wires and pipes and darkness and rust and confusion. No one would hear what happened down here. And who knew how long it would take for a person to be found. I suddenly remembered the shiv and bent down and pulled it from my sock and stuck it in my back pocket. *You can't use it*, I said to myself. *What are you thinking? You're just going to have to fist-fight him. He can't kill you. You can live through broken bones.*

I heard him coming down the steps. It didn't seem like it had been five minutes, but there was no way to tell. I saw his feet and then the rest of him, step by step, until his shoes slapped onto the wet floor. His face was twitching with excitement, but he wasn't smiling. I could imagine the hornets buzzing in his head.

"Hey, Jack," I said.

He didn't answer me.

"Listen, I—"

"Shut up."

He took another step toward me and cracked his knuckles. "You know what happened to the last guy I met down here?"

"No."

"They found him curled up over by that wall."

"I bet you're a lot of talk too."

"We'll see, won't we?"

"What's it gonna prove—you fightin' a new boy?"

"I'll fight anybody that disrespects me."

"What about Paco? You think he respects you? He thinks you're a coward."

"Hell with Paco."

"I wanna see you say that to his face."

"I don't have to deal with Paco. I don't have to deal with lots of things. You see, I know how Hellenweiler works. Not just the gangs, but the guards too. I've bought dirt on this place. I'll do just enough time to get by and they'll let me out. If they don't, I got people on the outside that'll speed things up. But you're gonna have to rot in this dog kennel."

"Yeah, what kinda dirt you got?"

"You'd like to know, wouldn't you?"

"Yeah, I would."

"Let's just say I can hurt you all I want and nobody outside of Hellenweiler will ever know a thing."

"You're that special, huh?"

"Oh, it has nothin' to do with me."

"What do you mean?"

"Why don't you stop stallin' and take this like a man?"

I felt my temper rising, and for once I was glad to feel it again. It welled up from my chest and smothered away any fear I'd had. This whole situation seemed like the biggest waste of anger and time and life I could imagine.

"I've never known people like you that didn't have it comin'," I said. "Sooner or later. Maybe I don't bring it, but somebody will."

"I spit on people like you."

"Well," I said, "I don't have a damn bit of respect for you either. Let's get this over with so I can curl up against that wall and get my ride out of here. I got people on the outside too. And I guarantee they can get drunker and meaner than your people. And their spit smells worse."

Jack took a step toward me. "Come on," he said. "You're not just gonna lay down on me, are you?"

"I ain't layin' down. I'm gonna make you earn every bit of this."

"Come on, then."

"Waitin' on you."

Then I saw his eyes go deep and calm. This was something he was savoring. He reached into his back pocket and his hand came away with a screwdriver. He held it low and put one foot before the other and rocked back and forth like someone about to sprint.

"Put it up," I said.

But I could tell in his eyes he was committed. Then I saw his arms tense and I knew it was coming. Without thinking about it, I went for the shiv just as he launched toward me.

When the lights went out, I was diving sideways. I felt the brush of Jack's body against me and heard him stumble and slide across the floor. I quickly got to my knees and searched the darkness for him. The blue light flickered and I saw him sitting up and staring at the staircase.

"What the—?" he said.

But there was no one there. Whoever had flipped off the lights had done it from somewhere else.

Jack stood and took a step toward the stairs. "Who's there?" he said.

But there was no reply. Just the sounds of the machines.

I tightened my grip on the shiv and started to stand. Before I could rise, another figure slipped out of the darkness behind Jack and pulled him to the floor. The room was suddenly filled with screaming. I backed against the cement wall in confusion. The blue flickering of the gas flames occasionally lit up the room enough for me to see the two dark shapes struggling not far from me. The sound of the machinery droned on and the two figures rose and fell and rolled like something displayed in a weak strobe light. The only human sounds were coming from Jack and they were nothing I could make out, only grunting and an occasional whimper of pain.

Then, after a few seconds of darkness, there was only one body left on the floor. I leaped up and ran for the stairs, feeling every hair on my neck standing at the thought of what was behind me. Whoever—whatever had attacked Jack. I took the steps two at a time and never looked back. When I got to the top, I threw the shiv on the floor and kept running. When I came to the door leading into the hall, I stopped and spun around and looked behind me. There was nothing. "Paco, you crazy Mexican," I said aloud.

* * *

90

I stood leaning with my forehead against the maintenance room door, catching my breath. The hall beyond was silent. I heard the boys in the rec room through the walls to my right and the faint plinking of dishes coming from the kitchen on my left. After a few minutes I opened the door and stepped out.

The hall seemed empty. Then I looked down at the entrance to the rec room and Preston stared at me with horror on his face. I locked eyes with him until he stepped out of sight. I shut the maintenance closet door and made for my bunk.

The floorwalker was gone. I lay on my bed and took deep breaths and replayed what had happened in the basement. But the whole scene was a blue, flickering nightmare that made no sense.

Later on, the floorwalker returned and the boys began filing in. The Ministers each had to pass by me to get to their end of the room. I didn't look at them, but I could feel their stares. Then I turned over and looked down at Paco's bunk. He was undressing at the foot of it. Just when I thought he wasn't going to acknowledge me, he turned his head and nodded and went back to what he was doing.

Caboose came in a few minutes later and rolled into his bed, the mattress springs creaking. I cocked my eyes at him but he paid me no attention.

That night no one came to talk to me. No one called me names. No one moved around much at all. I'd never seen the place so quiet.

"Where's number eighty-six?" I heard the floorwalker yell. That was Jack's number. No one spoke up.

"Where is eighty-six!" he yelled again.

Silence.

The floorwalker marched out of the room. A moment later I heard the guards rushing down the hall, locking the place down.

Next morning. I got in line for the showers. No one was speaking. I kept my eyes down and went through the routine of washing myself and returning to my bunk to get dressed. As I pulled on my jumpsuit, I noticed that Caboose was still in bed. His eyes were open and he seemed to be studying the underside of the top bunk. It was far past time for all the boys to be up and done with showers.

While I was making my bed, Mr. Pratt entered at the far end of the bunk room. He came our way, making his usual inspection walk. When he got to Caboose's bed, he stopped.

"On your feet, seventy-two!"

I continued making the bed, watching them in my periphery. Caboose didn't move. Mr. Pratt took a step toward him. "Christ," he said. I turned and saw him pull the radio from his belt. "John," he said, "I need a couple of guys to help me get seventy-two to the infirmary. We're in the bunk room. Hurry up."

I looked at Caboose's bed. I'd been on the other side of him earlier and hadn't noticed the blood staining his bedsheet and the entire side of his shirt.

18

We were all sent to breakfast early. When I was walking in the hall, I saw two guards rushing past with a stretcher. I turned and looked back at Paco. He studied me and made no expression.

I went to no-man's-land alone with my food. Leroy came first. He sat beside me and began eating without a word. Then the rest of them came, one by one. Until the entire table was filled with silent Ministers bent over their trays. At one point I looked up and glanced over my shoulder. Preston was the only one left. He kept his head down and ate alone.

"You're the leader now, Hal," Leroy said.

I didn't answer him.

When the buzzer sounded I took my tray and returned it. I headed for the recess yard and sensed them behind me. I stepped out into the sunlight and kept on until I was halfway to the fence. I saw the Hounds filing off toward their court on the right. When I stopped, the rest of the Ministers stopped. I turned and faced them. "That fence over there is my fence," I said. "Anybody that follows me is goin' to the boiler room."

"You don't have to stand by the fence anymore, Hal," Leroy said. "You can stay with us."

I ignored him. "Where's Preston?"

"He said he won't join us," one of the boys said.

"Go get the key to the boiler room from him. Put it under my pillow when we go back in. I keep it now."

"Then what should we do about him?"

"I figure he's got three places to go and he's gonna get his ass kicked in two of 'em. What you do with him is up to you."

Leroy looked at me with confusion. "What about us, Hal?"

"I don't know, Leroy. You guys figure it out without me."

I turned and left them.

I leaned against the fence and slid down it. I drew my knees up and studied the yard. The Ministers stood idle, talking among themselves, watching the Hounds. Preston appeared and stood near the entrance door next to Mr. Pratt.

I began to take the pieces of my situation and place them together. Caboose was the mysterious person in the boiler room. He did something to Jack and now both of them were hurt. I didn't know if Jack had been found. I didn't know if Paco was involved, but now he was the recognized leader of the entire yard and I felt safe for the time being. At least until Jack could tell everyone what had really happened. *If* he could tell them.

Paco came strolling toward me with the rest of the Hounds watching. He stood over me for a moment and then slid down the fence beside me.

"I didn't think you could be seen with me," I said.

"But we are equals now," he said. "We are two generals at a meeting."

"I don't have an army."

"So you say. But it doesn't matter. You have earned your respect. For the time being, you are untouchable."

I looked at him. I could tell. "You know what happened down there, don't you?"

"That doesn't matter either."

"So what's next?"

"Today we sit here on the hill and watch. Like good generals."

"Watch what?"

Paco gazed across the yard. Finally he said, "I had a friend on the outside. His father was a forester. One day he told me a story of how a big storm came through the woods and a violent wind tossed the tall pines back and forth all night. The next month, they found beetles in these trees that had always been healthy. You see, the timber was hurt. As you know, the inside of a tree is made of rings, each ring representing one year of growth. All of the tossing back and forth tore the bond between these rings in a process called delamination. The beetles are able to eat into a delaminated tree much easier. But the question was this: How did the beetles know the trees were wounded when they could not see the wounds?"

"I don't know, Paco."

"It is very interesting. You see, trees, like every animal, give off heat when they are sick. Just like you grow hot with fever. Lions can sense this in sick animals and they choose them to prey upon. The beetles sensed this as well."

"What do sick trees have to do with anything?"

Paco still stared across the yard. "Look at the Ministers. They are sick. And the dogs are sniffing them."

I studied the play yard, taking in both sides. I noticed there was a subtle tension building. The Ministers stood loose and idle on their basketball court. The Hounds were gathered in a tight group, talking among themselves and sneaking glances at their enemy.

"We are about to see something here," Paco said. "Something that has not been seen since Caboose took the fence a year ago."

"Caboose?"

He put his finger to his lips. "Watch," he said.

Mr. Pratt knew what was about to happen. There was no way he couldn't have seen it coming. But he turned his back and stepped inside the main building. When the door shut behind him, the group of huddled Hounds came apart and made a line, shoulder to shoulder. My eyes snapped over to the Ministers. Only one or two of them were watching the scene unfold, and even those seemed puzzled.

"They don't even know," I said.

"Lambs," Paco replied.

The Hounds began walking, the outside boys going a little faster so that a half circle was formed. Most of their prey would fall like fish into the center of the net and the strays would be caught by the wingmen. The arc made half the distance before the Ministers' expressions turned to looks of alarm. And the Hounds seemed to know it was time.

They didn't utter a sound as they rushed forward. All I heard was the dull digging of their rubber soles in the dry dust and the screaming of the Ministers. It was a blur of chaos and confusion as the Hounds descended on their cowering prey. My overall impression was of scar-banded wrists rising and falling in the midst of a dust storm. I watched with my mouth open and Paco silent beside me.

It seemed like the attack lasted for ten minutes but it was probably no more than two before Mr. Pratt swung open the door to the main building. He watched the scene patiently, tapping a nightstick against his palm. Finally he stepped down onto the yard. Behind him came three more guards, each of them with his own club. The men approached and entered the tangle of screaming boys. Then I saw their sticks rising and falling and caught glimpses of their faces, jaws clenched and eyes narrowed at the pleasure of what they dealt. I heard grunts of pain and more yelling. Boys began scattering in all directions. A few of them came against the fence not far from us and collapsed, their clothes torn and their faces covered in blood and dirt.

In the end, the guards stood in the settling dust. A few boys lay around them, moaning and curled into fetal positions.

"What the hell is this place?" I mumbled.

But Paco heard me. "It is home sweet home, my friend."

19

Once, when I was ten years old, Daddy lifted me out of bed before sunrise. Even though I was already tall for my age, it was no problem for him to carry me to the truck with my chin on his shoulder and my eyes closed. This was nothing unusual. It was late fall, hunting season, and he'd taken me to the woods with him since I was four.

He placed me on the passenger seat and shut the door. I pulled up my knees and leaned against the window. The rumble and workingman smell of his old truck, the one we still had at the clay pit, always comforted me. As we moved into the night I fell back into a slumber made deeper by his presence and the fact that I was included.

Some time later I woke to sunrise bleeding into the treetops. The truck was parked in the woods at the edge of a pond and I was alone. At first I was disoriented, then I vaguely remembered him placing me on the seat earlier.

I found him sitting on the bank of the pond, untangling a trotline from where it was wrapped messily around a block of wood. Beside him was a paper cup with hooks in it. On the other side of him was a bottle of whiskey. He always had whiskey and tobacco with him. It was part of his smell.

I sat next to him and rubbed my eyes and yawned. His hands continued to work at the tangle. Then I looked across the pond. "Where are we, Daddy?"

"One of Uncle Tom's lakes," he said without look-ing up.

Uncle Tom was Daddy's brother. He owned a pole mill in Livingston. He was rich, but never acted like it except on Christmas when he gave me nice presents.

I watched Daddy's fingers working at the knots. "Where's the bait?" I asked him.

"In the truck bed."

I got up and walked to the truck. I found a carton of chicken livers and started back. Before I reached him, he suddenly hurled the trotline into the brush.

"Forget it!" he said. "Stupid fish. What's the use!"

I stopped and watched his back. It wasn't like him to lose his temper. He turned and looked at me and I could see that he'd been crying. I'd never seen him cry before and it made me uncomfortable. "Just come here," he said calmly.

I went and stood next to him.

"Put it down. Sit down here."

I sat next to him while he unscrewed the top to his whiskey and took a drink. Then he set it to the side and put his arm around me and pulled me close. "We don't ever catch anything anyway, do we?"

I shook my head. We sat there for what seemed like a long time, staring across the still pond, watching the gum leaves drift down and settle around us. Crows called in the distance, and ever since then their sound taps a lonely place in me.

Daddy eventually pulled his arm away and reached for the whiskey. I stood and went to get the trotline. I sat down and worked at it while he drank. Eventually I freed the knots and brought it back to him. He pushed himself up and we spent the next hour baiting and stringing hooks across the pond. Then he got his .22 rifle from the truck and I followed him into the woods.

That morning we bagged a few squirrels and cleaned them at the truck. Then we drove to a country store nearby and bought souse and white bread and potato chips and chocolate milk and returned with it. We made sandwiches on the tailgate as the cool afternoon breezes lifted the hair on my head. Then we took a nap under a hickory tree. Late that afternoon we pulled in the trotline. There were no fish on it and every hook was still baited.

Just after sunset we packed our gear. Daddy took the last sip of his whiskey and threw the bottle into the truck bed and got behind the wheel. "Maybe next time," I said. Because that's what he always told me. And I smiled and watched his face.

He didn't answer me. He put the truck in gear and pulled away. After a few minutes he talked to me while he watched the road ahead. "I'm gonna drop you off at the house. I'm not gonna be stayin' at home anymore."

That day was the last time I remember being a happy boy.

Momma didn't want him. After he moved out of the house, he lived in a motel room for a while. Then he got the job at the clay pit about an hour away in Union. He tried to see me as much as he could on weekends, but Momma made it hard for him. She'd always have some excuse about things I had to do for school and such. But I wasn't doing anything. I was just waiting for my daddy. I just wanted him to come get me.

I got where I hated her and everything about where I lived. It wasn't long before I started skipping school. I'd get off the bus and hide under somebody's car in the parking lot. After classes started, I'd run off in the woods to a little farm pond about a quarter mile away and lie there and toss rocks in it and listen to the crows. Then I'd walk home as it got dark. The school would have already called, and she'd be pretty worked up by the time I walked through the door. For a while she took a switch to me. Then one day I realized I was bigger than she was, and I turned around and took the switch out of her hand and broke it and threw it to the ground. I told her if she ever switched me again I'd switch her back.

Then I let an older kid talk me into stealing bicycles for him. He'd pay me ten dollars a bike and that was more money than I'd seen. I'd walk into town at night and take them out of people's yards and bring them to an old barn in back of the kid's parents' house. I figured he sold them. I didn't care. It was a way for me to make money and get back at the world all at once.

I wasn't into the bike-stealing business long before the older kid got caught and turned me in. My mother was already fed up with me, and my reputation with the truancy officer didn't help my case. They sent me off to the Pinson Boys' Home.

Pinson was just a place where I could be mad and mean and get away with it. The oldest boys were almost fourteen, but I was already as big as all of them. And it didn't take much to set me off. I ruled that place. Nobody messed with me. Not until Moon Blake came along.

One night I was in the rec room and saw on television where they'd caught a ten-year-old kid that had been raised in the woods by his father. He was like an Indian. His dad kept him in a dugout way back in the forest where they hid out from everybody. The kid had never even met anybody but his dad and some storekeeper they went and saw a couple of times a year.

They bring him to Pinson and he's lying in his bunk with the covers pulled up over him like a trapped animal. I decided I'd go ahead and let him know who was in charge. He would've kicked my ass right then and there if one of the guards hadn't pulled him off me.

I went after him again a couple of days later and that time he did kick my ass. Laid me right out with a punch to the balls. I think back on that now and realize it was the best punch in the balls I ever got. I needed it. And I see this kid that's gone through more than I could even imagine and he's not about to let any of us get him down. Moon Blake taught me that no matter what life deals you or what you deal yourself, you can't stop trying. He showed me raw heart and courage. And even though he was a head shorter than me, I looked small next to him.

The day after our fight Moon came up and talked to me like we'd been friends forever. He wanted me to bust out of the boys' home with him. He had it all planned out like it was the simplest thing ever. And by that time, I would have followed him anywhere.

We escaped from Pinson, and for a while I had my life back. During the days we were on the lam, the world I'd given up on suddenly came out from behind the clouds. Eventually both of us ended up with Daddy and lived with him in the clay pit. The law finally caught us again, but it was all worth it. Those days with Daddy made me feel like a normal kid again.

I was eventually sent on to Hellenweiler. Before I left, Daddy and I made promises to go straight—him with the whiskey and me with the trouble. I knew it was going to be hard, but I never imagined it would be like this.

20

After the gang fight, Hellenweiler seemed like a different place. Everyone kept to themselves. Except for the
wrist scars and neck crosses, it would have been hard to
tell the difference between Ministers and Hounds. Paco
and I were the only boys without some sort of bandage.
The infirmary was so full that some of the residents had
to recover in their bunks.

Something told me that I should get rid of the key—
drop it down the shower drain or bury it in the yard—but
I didn't. I took it from beneath my pillow and hid it in my
stationery kit. Keeping control of it gave me a small sense
of security.

For a while, it was like Paco had lost interest in being
a Hound. He still sat at their table and I still sat alone in
no-man's-land, but he didn't pay attention to his gang and
they seemed too beat down to care. Out on the play yard,
it was never long before he strolled over and leaned against
the fence next to me and started his strange talks.

"Do you remember me telling you of my friend whose
father was a forester?"

"Yeah."

"He told me something else that I think about. He said
that his father believes that trees can communicate with
each other."

"Aww, come on."

"Listen to me. He said there was a grove of the same species of tree and a certain type of ant was eating the leaves from these trees. Let's say this grove was a circle and that the ants were eating on the middle trees. Over time, the trees on the outside of the circle developed a poison in their sap that the ants did not like. They changed their sap. How could they have known to do this?"

"I don't know. But I'll bet you have an idea about it."

Paco stared over the play yard and didn't answer me right away. Finally he said, "Yes. This place is poison."

I traced my finger across the dust and some time passed where we didn't speak. Then I said, "How'd you get here, Paco?"

He smiled to himself. "What have they told you?"

"Nothin'. I've never heard anything about it."

"That's unfortunate," Paco said. "I will need to ask one of the Hounds to remind me of what lie I told when I first came here. You see, the truth is not such a good thing in this place. Why did they send you here?"

"Stealin' bikes. Threatenin' my momma."

"Wrong answer, my friend. That answer serves you no purpose. Perhaps you are forgetting about the poor old man that you robbed and beat within one inch of his life before you took the bike."

"Maybe I should just shut up like Caboose."

Paco nodded. "Perhaps."

"So you won't tell me?" I said.

"It wouldn't matter. I am no longer the person I was. Now I am whatever they say I am. Whatever has been made of me."

"Somehow you got smart. That came from somewhere."

After a while he said, "I want to see the trees again."

"There's some across that mud field. Turn around and look at those."

"I want to smell them up close. I want to stand in their shade and hear the rustle of leaves. I want to pick an insect from the bark and let it crawl on my finger."

"I think you're crackin' up."

Paco shook his head in disagreement. "I could have been a forester."

"How old are you?"

"Seventeen," he said.

"You'll be out soon."

"Yes," he sighed. "I will. But you see what they have made of me. I am a gang leader. I am a bulldog. My only friends would be my enemies if they had the chance. That is what I know now. That is what they have taught me here."

"You're what you wanna be. You're what you always were."

"That is where you are wrong, my friend."

I waited for him to continue, but he didn't. He looked at his knees and thumped an ant from his jumpsuit.

"Who hurt Chase?" I finally asked.

"Do you know the Hound with all the ink?"

"Yeah, Tattoo?"

"His name is Carter Santos. He loves nothing more than an excuse to hurt people."

"I found that out in the confessional."

"There are boys in here like Tattoo and Jack. They are not made into violent people so much as they were born violent. It is genetic. You will often find that their fathers are the same way. Most people will say they are the most difficult to judge. I disagree. If you understand them, they are manageable. You see, they believe everyone must think the way they do. They believe they are the rule more than the exception. So you let them think that you are like them. And they will leave you alone. Behind that violence is always a seed of cowardice. They are all cowards."

"But not Caboose?"

Paco looked at me. "I will tell you about Caboose. And you will learn what you have failed to see about this place."

21

Paco slid down the fence and sat. I did the same and waited for him to tell his story.

"When I arrived here," Paco began, "Caboose was the leader of the Ministers. He was the one person no one touched. The Hounds were nothing but quivering cur dogs against the fence. It did not take me long to learn how the system works in this place. I saw an opportunity and picked my side wisely and took my fight. It was not difficult. The Hounds were weak and broken-spirited. I put a rock in my fist and walked up to their leader and hit him in the face with it until he fell to the ground and spit his teeth into the dirt. I have not been in a fight since. The Hounds regained their spirit when they saw what I had done to their leader. They straightened their backs and raised their voices and began to challenge the Ministers. I was ignorant and I enjoyed this."

"Did you think you could outfight Caboose?"

"Personally?"

"Yeah."

"Perhaps. I was foolish enough. But it didn't matter. I was a general, you see. I had no concerns."

"He could tear your arms off."

"You should listen to the rest of the story."

"Fine," I said. "Go on."

"So the Hounds became bold and agitated the Ministers. Day after day, the tension built. Then, one day, the Hounds attacked. It started much like what you witnessed a few days ago—silence and then the disappearance of the guard and then a rush. The dust rose in the yard and boys beat on one another. This went on until the guards came with their clubs. The boys are so worked up that they continue to fight and do not notice the guards. Perhaps even if they did notice they do not believe what is about to happen."

"So the guards attacked?"

"Yes. The clubs are rising and falling and the boys are screaming and crawling away. Soon it is over, and the guards have just about everyone that can walk or crawl up against the fence. But there are several boys lying on the ground. One of them is not moving. This is Marty. This is Caboose's younger brother."

"His younger brother?"

"Yes. Marty had come to Hellenweiler just before me."

"What did Caboose do?"

"He is kneeling beside his brother, screaming at him to get up, but it is the screaming of a person who already knows what he asks is impossible. And then I hear Mr. Pratt ask Caboose to move to the fence. And, you see, Mr. Pratt does this like a whisper to a roaring lion. And he only says this once. Of course Caboose does not leave his brother. And this is what they want, you see. Like me, he had been a spectator and they had no excuse to beat him. But now he does not hear them. So the guards close in and I hear the clubs hitting his back like punches to a side of beef. Slowly, after many blows, Caboose becomes silent. But he remains there like a cow gone to his knees. Then, after many more blows, he rolls over and falls across his brother."

"That's crazy," I said.

"They took them away. Two weeks later, only Caboose returns. He walks into the yard and crosses to this fence where you and I are sitting now."

"The guards killed his little brother?"

"Yes, my friend. Now you know about Caboose. And now you know what it is you have failed to realize. You see, it is not the Hounds and the Ministers you should be afraid of. They are simply cowards at their little games. They have no real power. It is the people who make them what they are. It is the adults here. Mr. Fraley and his guards."

"Paco, how can they do this? Why don't the guards stop the fights?"

"As long as we fight, we are considered to be violent juveniles, not fit to leave this place. They take notes. They record it all. They allow little skirmishes to take place here and there. Occasionally they let the gangs go at each other to perpetuate the tension. Fatten the reports. That is what Mr. Fraley wants. He feels his duty as a public servant is to keep the stray dogs off the streets."

"How can he just cover all this up?"

"He walks a very fine line with this policy, my friend. It is a complicated situation. You see, too many injuries and the home is suspect. So they must be careful about who they send to the hospital and what they report."

"But Chase went. And I guess Jack and Caboose went."

"Yes. I suppose they can get away with a few. That is expected in this place that encourages violence. Unpreventable. But they must be careful."

"Isn't there at least one honest guard in this place?"

"What is honest? We choose to fight each other. There are many ways they can interpret this."

"Is Jack dead?"

"No."

"How do you know."

"Because I know."

"He'll be back, won't he?"

"Probably. He is not capable of staying out of trouble. He is a true violent criminal. But I suppose his lawyers will get him out for a while when he whimpers to his father that he has been abused."

I wanted to ask Paco why Caboose defended me, but I still wasn't sure what he knew.

"What if I'm not gone before Jack walks onto this yard again?"

"What do you do when you go to cut down a tree?"

I rolled my eyes. "Here we go again."

"You study it. You see how it leans, what it might fall on. Where the knots are. Then you cut it down."

"That really helps, Paco."

"You can't control the adults, but you can manipulate the boys. You need to stop thinking about getting out and continue to learn about staying in. Study the boys. Learn what makes them fall. Anticipate the effect their fall will have on the things around you."

The buzzer sounded and Paco sighed and got to his feet. "Another day in paradise, my friend."

I got up. "Yeah. Hopefully there won't be many more."

After classes on Friday I waited for Paco. He mingled with the Hounds for a few minutes and then strolled over to me. This time he didn't lean against the fence. "I'm afraid our meetings must come to an end," he said. "The dogs are getting suspicious. They are starting to talk."

"All right."

"I think the boys will leave you alone for a while. And your secret is safe with me."

I didn't respond.

"There is a standing invitation for you to join the Hounds, but I know you will not accept it. Therefore, I wish you well. You understand I have an investment to protect?"

"Yeah, I get it. So that's it?"

"I'm afraid so."

"See you around then."

Paco stared at me for a moment, then turned and left. I watched him cross the yard and fall in with the Hounds. Then I was alone again.

22

Daddy came to see me on Saturday. Carla wasn't with him.

"Her daddy wouldn't let her come, would he?" I said.

"I just didn't have time to pick her up."

"That's a lie. She's too good for me and everybody knows it."

"I'm about to whop you on the head, boy."

"Go ahead, it won't hurt me."

Daddy stared at me for a second.

"What?" I finally said.

A big goofy grin spread across his face. "Mr. Wellington said he thinks you'll be out real soon. The judge looked at everything and thinks we've held up our end of the deal."

I sat up in my chair. "Bull!"

"Keep it down, son. You wanna get hauled out of here?"

"You go see him?"

"Yeah. He'd already talked to Judge Mackin, and the only thing left to do is get your paperwork from Hellenweiler. He's already put in the call."

"I been clean since the day I got here."

"He don't see any problems. Says Judge Mackin never really wanted you to come here in the first place. Said you proved to be a real man when you turned yourself in after the escape."

"Then why'd he even send me? Hell."

"A judge has to follow the law, son. You want me to get onto him about it?"

I smiled and looked down at the tabletop. "No. Man, I just wanna go fishin', Daddy. I just wanna get in the truck and take some dirt road somewhere. Maybe go down to Uncle Tom's lake. Take Carla with me."

Daddy listened and nodded.

"Just start all over and do it right," I said.

"Where is everybody, today? This place is dead quiet."

"There was a big fight between a couple of gangs about a week ago. It's been pretty slow around here since then."

"You did good to stay out of it."

"You don't even know. I'll be glad to get away from all of this."

Daddy stood to go. "I wish we could visit more today. Things have picked up at the clay pit and I can't stay gone long."

I stood. "All right," I said.

Daddy grabbed my hand and we shook. "Hang in there, boy. We're almost done."

Dear Carla,

Daddy came by and saw me today. He said my lawyer might have me home in a week. I'm going to be straight as a preacher when I get out. I doubt I'll be driving the truck on the blacktop again until I'm sixteen, but I figure I can get Daddy to bring me by

your house. Maybe you could get your sister to take
us out sometime. Anyway, I just wanted you to know
that I'm coming home.

Love,
Hal

I addressed the envelope and sealed it and set it aside. I
heard someone enter the bunk room and looked up to see
Leroy coming toward me. I lay back and waited for him.

"Hey, Hal," he said sheepishly.

"Hey, Leroy."

He stopped before my bunk and looked around to make
sure we were alone. "You doin' okay?" he asked.

"Yeah. Real good. I'm gettin' out of here next week. I
just wrote Carla about it."

Leroy looked at the floor. His forehead still had a bruise
on it from the gang fight.

"What'd she say to you when she sent you that letter,
anyway?"

Leroy shook his head.

"Better not have been any kind of love note," I said.

"She said to make sure you didn't get in trouble."

I smiled. "After you already kicked my ass."

Leroy nodded. "I wanted to tell you I was sorry about
that. About all of it."

"I know. Don't worry about it. This place makes you do
crazy things."

"I wish you were our leader. If it's not you, it's going to
be Preston."

I didn't answer him. He looked up at me again. "Preston doesn't believe you beat up Jack in the basement. He's tryin' to tell us it was all a trick."

"What do you think?"

"I don't care. Most of the boys are tired of all the fightin'. I just want it to stop."

"It ain't gonna stop. Preston thinks he's got somethin' to prove. And the guards won't help you."

"You wanna go out on the play yard with me?"

"Go ahead," I said. "You don't need to be seen with me."

"I don't think I care anymore."

"I'm gonna be out of Hellenweiler soon anyway. Maybe one day when both of us are on the other side of that fence things'll be different."

"Will you write to me?"

"Sure."

Leroy looked at his feet again and nodded.

"Go ahead," I said again. "I'll be out there in a little while."

23

After Moon and I turned ourselves in, Judge Mackin gave me one last week of freedom before they sent me off to Hellenweiler. Moon went down to Mobile to live with his new family and I was left alone at the clay pit with Daddy. I'd been outside the fence for three months, mud-riding, shooting guns, chewing tobacco, and doing pretty much whatever I wanted. I had the time of my life. But the morning after Moon left, I woke up feeling pretty empty and worthless.

Daddy wasn't much for doing laundry, so I decided to make myself useful and take our dirty clothes and bed-sheets up the road to the Laundromat. We had our own washer and dryer at the clay pit, but they were lying in the backyard, gutted and rusted and tipped over for doghouses.

I was leaning against the wall, waiting for a load to dry, when I first saw Carla. She came in with her sister, Rhonda, and they shook their laundry into one of the machines and sat down in the chairs to wait. She was the best-looking girl I'd ever seen and I couldn't stop watching her.

After a few minutes Rhonda got up and went to the service station next door to get a Coke. Carla grabbed a magazine from the chair next to her and started to flip through it. I tried to find excuses for why I shouldn't talk to her, but I knew that this might be my last chance until I was eighteen.

I made like I was looking for something and walked her way. I didn't know why I was nervous. My hands were shaking so much I had to jam them down in my pockets. I felt my mouth drying up and hoped I'd be able to talk without sounding like a frog.

"You seen any blue jeans lyin' around?" I asked her.

She looked up from the magazine and shook her head. I tried to think of something else to say. "What's your name?"

She gave me a funny look. "Carla," she said.

"I'm Hal. That's my truck outside the window."

She turned and looked at it. Then she did this thing with her eyes where she crinkles them up and almost laughs. "You're not old enough to drive," she said.

"Well, you see it out there, don't you?"

"I bet your daddy's next door."

"You watch this," I said.

I walked outside, got in the truck, cranked it, and revved it a couple of times so she could hear my muffler I'd drilled a few holes in. Then I threw it in reverse and peeled out backward onto the blacktop. I looked at her and she was still watching me. I worked the column shifter and popped the clutch and squalled the tires for twenty feet before they caught and shot me down the highway. After I'd gone about a hundred yards I turned around in the ditch and came back and parked right in front of her again. She was laughing behind the window glass. I didn't expect that.

When I stepped inside again, she had tears in her eyes. "You're crazy," she said.

I didn't like her laughing at me. "You still wanna bet on my daddy?"

She wiped her eyes and shook her head. "No," she laughed. "I believe you."

"You wanna go for a ride?"

She dropped her mouth open like it was the craziest idea she'd ever heard. "Not with you!"

"Why not?"

"Because you don't have a license!"

I took a deep breath and looked out the window, hoping Rhonda wouldn't come out.

"What if I get my daddy to take us on a date?"

"I don't even know your name."

She was making me mad. "Hal," I said.

She laughed again.

"Look, I ain't got but a week before I go off to school. Maybe we could just go fishin' or somethin'."

"Okay," she said.

I couldn't believe it. "Really?"

"Sure. My daddy's Gant Hartley. He's in the phone book."

I told Daddy I'd met a girl I wanted to take out and he offered to drive us to the dirt track races on Saturday night. I'd never been to the dirt track and I'd never been on a real date. I put on my best jeans and a Waylon Jennings T-shirt and slicked my hair back and even dabbed on a little Canoe aftershave that I found in Daddy's dresser drawer.

"Lady-killer," he said.

"Shut up."

We drove to Carla's house and I went inside and talked to her parents and figured I made a pretty good impression. They didn't know anything about where I'd been and where I was headed and I wasn't about to tell them. Finally Carla came out from a back room like they'd been keeping her until I passed inspection. She looked even better than I remembered.

I don't know if it was the race cars or the girl or both, but that night got to me like a place I never wanted to leave. Carla sat close to me and leaned into my shoulder whenever the noise of the race car engines got too loud. And they were loud. Their vibrations came up through the cement bleachers and shook your bones. Carla clung to me and I couldn't keep my eyes off what was going on. For the first time in my life, I knew what I wanted to be if I could ever get untangled from the law.

"I wanna race those late models one day," I told her.

"I'll bet you'd be good."

"Yeah," I said.

The rest of that week was hard. It was tough to see Daddy look at me like he did—for a long time, like every time was the last. But mostly it was hard to see all the things I wanted that I couldn't have. Things that were just going to go away like they never were. Like Daddy. Like Carla. Like becoming a dirt-track racer.

I drove to Carla's house a couple of nights during the week and parked down the road. She snuck out of her window and met me. We'd sit on the tailgate and talk. Sometimes I'd play the truck radio low and she'd get up behind me and put her hands in my back jeans pockets and we'd rock back and forth. Daddy cared for me, but I knew this was a whole different kind of thing. Carla liked me and she was proud of me and she believed in me. But she still didn't know the truth.

The night before I left, we sat on the tailgate swinging our legs and listening to country music and drinking a couple of hot Budweisers I'd found in the toolbox. We didn't talk much at first. I felt sick over everything she didn't know about me. I knew I had to come clean.

"I ain't really goin' off to school tomorrow," I finally said. "Not regular school anyway."

She pulled away from me and studied my face.

"I gotta go away to juve."

"Like jail?"

"Yeah, pretty much."

"What'd you do?"

"Stole some bikes a long time ago. Skipped school. Gave Momma a hard time."

She asked me a lot of questions and I stared at my shoes and just about told her my whole life story. And it felt good to tell somebody besides Daddy about it all. Because there were some things I couldn't talk to him about. Like how I didn't really think he could stop drinking and how bad I'd treated my mother.

"I don't care," she finally said.

I stopped swinging my feet and looked away from my shoes. Her face was right there and I leaned into her and kissed her on the mouth. Her lips were soft and tasted like cherry ChapStick. I'd been thinking about that kiss ever since.

121

* * *

The next morning Officer Pete came to pick me up at the clay pit. He waited outside in his cruiser while I sat on the kitchen counter feeling gut-shot.

"I can't do this, Daddy."

"Yeah you can. It's just for a little while. You remember what Mr. Wellington told us. You and me keep it between the lines and he'll spring you loose."

"You gotta do it, Daddy. You got to."

"I know. Soon as you leave here I'm gonna clean this trailer of every bottle of whiskey, empty or full, and throw 'em in that clay pit."

I looked at the floor, nodded, and slid off the counter.

"Look at me, son."

I did. He put his arm around me and pulled me close and squeezed me hard. "Let's walk on out there," he said.

24

Saturday afternoon Mr. Pratt came for me on the play yard. "Mr. Fraley wants to see you," he said.

I followed him to the door leading into the administrative offices. He opened it and ushered me inside. "You know where to go," he said.

I went to Mr. Fraley's office and knocked and waited until he told me to enter. When I opened the door, he sat behind his desk with his feet up and his hands crossed in his lap.

"Henry Mitchell," he said like he'd been thinking about me. "How are you?"

"I'm fine."

He motioned me closer. I stepped up to the red line and stopped.

"Did you enjoy visiting with your father?"

There was something menacing about the way he spoke to me. I nodded slightly.

"You know, I had a call from your lawyer yesterday. He tells me the judge is considering letting him regain custody of you."

"Yessir."

"The judge wants me to send him your conduct report."
I nodded.

"All of that is fine and good. Just part of the system."

He took his feet down and swiveled in his chair so that he faced the wall of books. "You may recall our conversation when you first arrived here," he continued. "I'm afraid I wasn't as clear as I should have been. I spoke to you about the uselessness of teaching and reforming the dogs. But that is only the problem. The solution is what I am paid for. You know what that is?"

I shook my head.

"Well, let me create a picture for you. When somebody leaves the garbage at the end of their driveway to be picked up, they have been told that it will go into a nice landfill. And over time this landfill will be manipulated and transformed into something pleasing. It will be smothered with fresh dirt and green grass will grow on the top. Soon it will become a beautiful golf course. The problem will go away. You see, this is what they tell you. This is what you want to hear. Well, the garbagemen know this is not true. And deep down, *you* know it is not true. The garbage will always be there. You cannot get rid of it. You can only hide it. And you can be glad that the fine, dedicated public servants that take away your trash continue to do what they do. You see, I am such a public servant. A servant with the thankless job of keeping our streets clean. Free of the stray dogs. The people really want nothing more. They do not want the details."

"I'm not like I used to be," I said.

"Is that so?"

I nodded.

Mr. Fraley reached into his desk and pulled out the shiv Paco gave me and I felt the blood rush to my face. He held it up before me. "Did you make this?"

"Nossir."

Mr. Fraley studied me for what seemed like a full minute. Then he set the shiv on his desk and opened my jacket and wrote something in it.

"What'd you write?" I asked him.

"That's none of your business."

"I didn't make it. I haven't fought anybody."

"No?"

I shook my head.

He leaned back in his chair and folded his hands across his lap. "I have all kinds of boys here. White, black, Mexican, young, and old. They are all in here for different reasons. But you know what every one of them has in common?"

I didn't respond. My mouth felt dry and I was feeling light-headed.

"They are liars. Every one of them. The first thing they will tell me when accused of something is that they didn't do it. But you see, that's just part of the whole process. It is expected. Then I have to investigate, which is fine. I'm paid for it."

"I'm not a liar."

Mr. Fraley ignored me and continued. "So you see, I ask Caboose who stabbed him, and of course he says nothing. And then the guards find Jack in the basement and I think I have the answer. But these things are not always as they seem. I know that. And I go to investigate the situation myself. I find this weapon in the utility corridor. Then I walk down into the basement and I find where Jack was lying in his blood. And leading out the back is another blood trail. So I ask myself, if Jack lies on the floor and there is a blood trail leading out the back, how did this weapon come to be in the utility corridor?"

He studied me. I didn't answer him. Finally he reached in his desk again and pulled out a key and set it beside the shiv. It could have been any key, but I knew exactly which one it was and my vision blurred over it. "We'll go to question two," he said, his voice suddenly sounding far away. "Did you steal the key that I found in your locker? The one that opens the maintenance closet where I found the shiv?"

I felt my knees growing weak. "Nossir."

He wrote something else down. "What'd you write?" I asked him again. But he ignored me.

"I didn't fight anybody," I said. "I didn't make the shiv. I didn't steal the key. I've tried to go by the rules."

Mr. Fraley looked at the sheet of paper on his desk. "But that's not what this conduct report says."

"You can't do that!" I yelled.

He twitched slightly in his chair, but his empty expression was set in stone. Then I heard the door open behind me, but I didn't turn around. I knew it was a guard. Mr. Fraley's hand came up and signaled him back.

"Mr. Pratt tells me the boys are quite fond of you now. That's good. You should think of them as your brothers."

"The hell I will! This ain't my family!"

"Take him to solitary, Mr. Pratt."

I felt the hand on my shoulder. I tried to twist away and the fingers dug clawlike into my collarbone and pain shot up my neck. Then I was hit hard from behind and I went to my knees with the room spinning. I winced as Mr. Pratt

126

twisted one of my arms behind my back and pulled up against it. "You understand what I'm sayin' to you, boy?" Mr. Pratt said.

I rose with my shoulder feeling like it would dislocate at any second. "That's right," he said. "Real easy now."

I took one last glance at Mr. Fraley. He was already looking back at his desk.

Mr. Pratt turned me over to one of the other guards and I was led down the hall. My mind was numb and blank. I couldn't believe what was happening to me. He took me past the rec room and then right and paused to unlock the big black doors. Then we entered another short hall and across from us were eight single doors with slots in the center. He led me to one of them and unlocked it and shoved me inside.

The seg cells were no bigger than closets. The only things in them were a stainless steel toilet, sink, and mattress on the floor. The air smelled of pee and puke and the cinder-block walls were smeared and finger-wiped with food and snot. Fluorescent lights hummed and flickered overhead.

The door clanged shut behind me and locked.

I lay on the mattress with panic pulsing in my temples and pounding away my ability to think straight. It was like I'd been climbing this cliff ever since I'd come to Hellenweiler, and just when I was about to reach the top, someone had kicked me off the ledge. Now I lay at the bottom and I didn't think I had the strength to try again.

25

There was no way to tell how much time had passed. The lights never went out and they needled my ears with their electric humming. Sometimes I heard coughing in the room next to me. Once, I heard the outside door unlock, and the sound and shadow of footsteps passed before the small crack at the base of my cell door. Then the guard left and the door locked behind him.

At some point I slept and then woke to the clattering of a food tray being shoved into the slot. I got up and pulled it the rest of the way through. I took off the cover and saw breakfast.

I sat on the floor and ate while I listened to the guard continue down the short hall. I heard him unlock the door of the cell next to me and enter it. "You want it?" he said.

There was no reply. The door closed and locked again and the guard left. I chewed slowly and listened. Nothing.

I put the empty food tray back in the slot and lay down again. After a while the guard came back, took it away, and left again without stopping at the other cell.

After a few minutes I heard a scratching sound outside my door. I sat up and stared at the crack near the floor. A small, broken piece of mirror tied to a thread was lying just inside the room. I got up and went to it and untied it and studied it. Then I remembered what Paco had told me about using the plastic to talk to the person next to you. I stuck it out the food slot and focused it down the hall. There was a large arm sticking from the slot in the cell next to me. The arm held the other half of my broken mirror.

"Caboose?" I said.

His meaty face stared back at me.

"I thought you were in the hospital," I said to the mirror.

"It takes more than a stab wound to leave this place," he mumbled. It was strange to hear words coming from his mouth. He spoke softer than I imagined.

"Why'd you help me?"

"You wouldn't have made it."

"Now you're in trouble."

"I was already in trouble. There's no tellin' what they've put in my jacket."

"Why don't you say anything out there?"

"Because it won't help. You might as well lay down and let them make you what they want."

"Paco tells me the same thing. And I think it's crap."

"Paco's smart. Smarter than anybody in here."

"What did he do?"

Caboose coughed. Finally he said, "I don't know. It doesn't matter."

"They've messed with my file too. I'm in here for all kinds of stuff now. I don't think they're gonna let me out."

"You're right. They won't."

"How can they do this?"

"It doesn't matter."

"The hell it doesn't!"

Caboose watched me in the mirror for a moment and then I saw his arm pull away and the corridor was empty.

"Where you goin'?"

"To lay down."

"Man, I just got you talkin'. Don't go layin' down on me."

He didn't answer.

"Fine," I said. "Talk to me without the mirror. How long will they keep us in solitary?"

"I'll be here until this stab wound gets better. They'll prob'ly let you out tomorrow."

"This place ain't so bad. If I wasn't so pissed, I'd kick back and relax for once. Why does everybody throw a hissy fit back here?"

"Sometimes they leave you in for days. People go crazy. Get sick on the floor. The guards don't clean it up."

"To me it's all the same inside the fence. They can keep me in a cardboard box for all I care. I just gotta get home, Caboose. I don't know how much more of this I can take."

"You'll make it."

"It's like a nightmare."

"When you have the same nightmare over and over it's not so scary anymore. I gotta rest."

"All right. But when we get out of here, you gotta stop clammin' up on me in the yard. I know you can talk now."

He didn't answer me.

"None of this lookin' at your feet," I said. "I know they stink, but starin' at 'em ain't gonna do any good."

After the guards delivered lunch and left, I listened to Caboose scraping his plate.

"You must be feelin' better," I said.

He didn't answer me.

"You lookin' at your feet again?"

"You talk too much."

"Somebody's gotta start talkin'. We gotta figure some-thin' out, Caboose."

Caboose was silent.

"What would you do if you could get out of here?"

"You don't wanna know."

"Yes I do."

"I don't want you to talk to me anymore. I need to rest."

"What about when we get out in the play yard again?"

He didn't answer me.

"Fine," I said. "But I ain't takin' this crap!"

26

I lay on my mattress that afternoon, staring at the dirty walls, trying to think through the anger running hot in my head. I told myself that I was going to work things out. I just needed to see Daddy and Mr. Wellington. I needed to tell them what Mr. Fraley was doing to me. But after a while the anger melted into a feeling of helplessness that seeped through me like poison. *Who was I to think that I could get around the system here when everyone else had failed? I'd never been the smartest kid in any group. I didn't have money. Maybe Caboose and Paco were right. It was all hopeless. There was nothing else to do but wait until you were eighteen.* I rolled over, hugged my knees to my chest, and stared at the wall. Images of Jack standing in the strange light of the boiler room flashed through my head. The evil in his eyes and the confidence on his face. And I kept hearing the words he spoke: *I can hurt you all I want and nobody outside of Hellenweiler will ever know a thing.* I closed my eyes and tried to forget it all.

I dreamt of being lost in the boiler room. This time it was a blue flickering maze as big as a football field with the machinery screaming in my ears. I was running, trying to find my way out. Jack was somewhere behind me. I could hear his feet slapping the water on the floor. Whenever I looked over my shoulder I caught the glint of a kitchen knife in his hands. But I couldn't find my way out. Every turn I took there were more of the screaming machines. And he was getting closer. And closer.

I opened my eyes and stared at the overhead lights. My breathing was heavy and my mind raced with the fading memory of the nightmare. I waited until my head cleared and the other nightmare, the real one, sat on me like a carcass.

"Caboose," I said.

No response. I started to call his name again, but didn't. He wouldn't have any answers. It was just me now. There had only been one other time in my life when I'd felt so alone.

The Talladega National Forest seemed an endless expanse of rolling green hills. Two of us followed Moon Blake miles into the thick of it after we escaped from Pinson. We were going to use Moon's survival skills to live in the wild and be free again.

Kit was a sick kid that knew he didn't have long to live. I was just looking for another way to trouble the system. But once we were living on our own there wasn't anybody or anything left for me to fight. I started thinking less about what others wanted of me and more of what I wanted of myself. For the first time in years I was rid of all the junk in my head and the adults in my face. And I wanted to see Daddy.

Moon didn't want me to leave them, but he understood why I had to do it. His dad was dead and he missed him every day. I set out one morning with two bloodhounds that were with us, and I headed home to the clay pit.

I faced a cold, wet forest that seemed to stretch endlessly in every direction. Moon had told me to follow water and I would eventually get to a road. I fought briars and tangles of kudzu, sometimes crawling on my stomach. The dogs never seemed to tire and were always up ahead waiting patiently for me, encouraging me to keep on. At one point I slipped down the bank and plunged into the creek and swirled in its blurry depths. I thought it was all over for me. The icy water gripped me like a cold fist while I struggled to find my footing. Finally I broke the surface and thrashed my way to the bank where I snatched at roots and tree limbs until I could finally pull myself out.

I didn't know how to make a fire, so I kept moving behind the dogs to stay warm. The forest loomed over me, darker and crueler than ever. My mind was numb to everything except following the dogs and fighting my way through the tangle of the creek bottom.

Late afternoon I came to a deep ravine and there was no way to follow the water except from above. I climbed out and caught up with the dogs and lay down in the pine needles to rest. I stared at the sky and wondered how much farther I had to go and if I had it in me to make it. Then I wondered if I was even going in the right direction. The weight of these thoughts sat on me until I was so confused and lonely that I wanted to turn around and find my friends again. But the woods were growing dark and settling into an eerie twilight stillness. I felt like the forest creatures were crouched and watching me with yellow eyes. I was too scared to move. I backed against a tree and pulled the dogs close to me and cried. I hadn't cried since the day Daddy drove away from Momma's house with his stuff stacked up in back of the truck.

Night set in and I lay with my eyes open, balled tightly in my damp clothes, feeling the warmth of the dogs breathing against me. Even if I hadn't been cold and wet and hungry, fear would have kept me awake. I stared up through the pine canopy at the clear night sky and a sliver of moon. I might as well have been standing up there, as alone as I felt. Every part of me knew this was no place I was meant to be.

My eyes were still open when the forest purpled with daybreak. I felt my courage build as each dark shape revealed itself in the light. Finally I stood and the dogs rose and stretched beside me. "I don't guess anybody's comin' to carry me out of here," I said to them. "Hell with this place."

I didn't take but a few steps before I broke out onto an old tram road that ran the high ground above the creek. I'd stumbled upon a path out of the forest. I wished I'd found it earlier, but there it was.

I still had those dogs waiting on me at the clay pit. They'd done all they could to help me. But it had always been up to me. I was the only help I had.

27

I rolled off the mattress and got to my feet.

"Caboose!" I yelled.

No answer.

I searched for the mirror, found it, and stuck it out the slot. The corridor was empty and quiet. Then I heard him say, "What?"

"Stick the mirror out and talk to me."

After a minute I saw Caboose's arm appear from the slot. Then I saw his face in the mirror.

"I gotta get out," I said. "I gotta go home. I came too far for this."

"I can't keep gettin' up. The stab wound bleeds when I move too much."

"They lied about me! They can't do this to me!"

Caboose didn't reply.

"They're stealin' my life! I'll be damned if I'm gonna play by anybody's rules when the guards let me out of this dog box."

Caboose's arm withdrew.

"Fine," I said. "Go ahead and lay down. I'm gonna get my own dirt on these people if it's the last thing I do."

I pulled my arm back in and sat on the floor. "This ain't happenin'. No way in hell. They ain't seen trouble until they've seen what I can bring 'em."

* * *

A guard came for me late Monday morning. He escorted me by the arm from solitary, and we stepped into the hall again and the familiar smell of disinfectant and bleach rushed into me.

"How'd you like seg?" he sneered.

"I don't know what all the yellin's about. You're gonna have to do better than that if you wanna impress me."

He stopped and looked down at me. "You wanna be a smart-ass?"

"I don't see what difference it'd make."

He let go of my arm and hit me across the back of the head. I took a step forward and got my balance. Then I turned and looked up at him and locked eyes. I thought he would hit me again, but a smile slowly spread across his face. "Thata boy," he said. "Now Mr. Pratt's really gonna have a good time with you. Get out of here. Stay in the bunk room until lunch."

I lay on my bed until I heard the others file into the hall when class let out at noon. After they passed and everything was quiet, I slid off my bunk and went after them.

The mess room was louder than I remembered. Things were getting back to normal since the gang fight. Preston was sitting in Jack's old chair at the Ministers' table and he glanced at me a few times as I got my food. Leroy gave me a half smile and I nodded at him.

I faced the Hounds while I ate. Paco tipped his fork at me discreetly and I raised my cup and twitched it in response. "That's right, you crazy Mexican," I mumbled. "I'm back. I'm back and pissed off."

* * *

Preston approached me on the play yard the next day. He was eating a candy bar from the canteen. I remained leaning against the fence and watched him until he stopped before me. "What do you want?" I said.

"You know the Ministers need a leader?"

"I don't care what they need."

"They want me to be their leader if you won't do it."

"Fine. Be their leader."

He studied me for a second. "I'd like to hear Jack's side of what happened down there."

"What's your point, Preston?"

"I just don't know how you did it. He's bigger and meaner than you."

"You want me to show you?"

He didn't reply.

"Then go on over there and be the leader and play your stupid little game."

"We'll be strong again. We've got some tough guys."

"Good for you," I said.

"They'll forget about what you did after a while."

"Maybe I'll come kick your ass and remind 'em."

Preston started to say something, but didn't. He shifted his feet nervously, then turned and started walking back.

"And the next time you get in my face," I said after him, "I'm gonna lay you out."

He kept walking like he didn't hear me.

"Yeah, you heard right, you little wuss. Just try me. I don't have anything to lose anymore."

28

Daddy looked bad when I saw him on Thursday. His eyes were red and I don't think he'd showered in a few days.

"You didn't start up again, did you?"

He shook his head. I held out my hand to him and he grabbed it limply. "They ain't gettin' away with this crap," I said.

We sat across from each other. "What happened?" he asked me. "I thought it was all clean."

"They lied to Mr. Wellington. I didn't do any of it. This place is illegal as hell."

"What are you talkin' about, son?"

"I'm talkin' about the people that run this place do whatever they want and tell people on the outside a whole 'nother story."

"Mr. Wellington said they've got you written up for knife fightin'."

"That's a damn lie too."

"He doesn't know what he can do."

"I know. But I'll tell you one thing, I ain't sittin' back and lettin' this happen, Daddy. I'm through playin' by the rules. I ain't never done a bit of good in my life, but I'm about to start."

"You ain't doin' nothin'. If there's some ass-kickin' that needs to be done, I'll do it."

"They ain't gonna let me out of here before I'm eighteen."

"You need to watch your temper."

"Screw my temper. Get Mr. Wellington to come see me. I need to talk to him. I need to tell him what I know."

Daddy started to say something, but stopped himself. "Okay," he said. "I'll see if I can get him over here."

"And don't you start drinkin' again. Whatever they said, I been keepin' my side of our deal. For now, at least."

Daddy nodded. I clenched my jaw and breathed heavy out of my nose and tried to calm myself.

"Don't tell Carla about all this."

"I won't."

"Maybe you can go ahead and get Moon's address for me."

"I can do that. You said you wanted to give him a little more time to adjust to his new family."

"Yeah, I know. He'd probably try and come bust me out or somethin'. Forget it."

"You sure?"

"Yeah, forget it. He'd know by my letters I was in trouble. He don't need that right now."

"Well, I'll work on it anyway and you'll have it when you're ready. I'm sure he'd like to hear from you."

I put my hand through my hair and looked around and took a deep breath.

"You know," he continued, "I told you things picked up at the clay pit. Got that new construction project up the road. We're tryin' to hire another driver, but they want me to work overtime until we get somebody. I might not be able to come by as much until we do."

"That's fine. You need to keep your job and stay straight. I'll be all right."

"Well, you know I'm thinkin' about you every day."

"I know."

I was surprised to hear I had a visitor Saturday morning. When I entered the visiting room I saw Mr. Wellington waiting for me at a side table. Off to my left I saw Paco sitting and talking quietly with a small, neatly dressed man. The man had Paco's round face.

Mr. Wellington didn't have his briefcase with him that morning.

"That was pretty fast," I said, sitting across from him.

He smiled politely, but I could see the disappointment in his eyes. "Your father said you wanted to see me."

I looked around the room. A guard stood against the far door, biting his fingernails and studying his hand. "There anyplace we can talk in private?" I asked.

"I'm not sure that would help. I don't know what else I can do for you, Hal. I'm sorry."

I leaned in close to him. "They lied to you, Mr. Wellington. I know it's hard to believe comin' from a guy like me, but they flat out made it all up."

"All of it?"

"All of it. You gotta believe me."

"It doesn't matter what I believe, Hal. I've seen the conduct report. That's the evidence."

"It's all a lie."

"Can you prove it?"

"I don't know how. How would I do it?"

He shook his head.

"This place is so corrupt you wouldn't believe it. They got boys that need to be in the hospital and they won't let 'em go."

"What do you mean?"

"I mean, I know a guy that got stabbed in here. They just wrapped him up and stuck him in solitary until he got better."

"Why would they do that?"

"I don't know. This whole place is screwed up."

"The state would investigate if there was an unusually high rate of injury."

"But not if they cover it all up and don't report it."

"Hal."

"What?"

"You're going to have to start accepting your situation."

"Don't start that, Mr. Wellington. You got to listen to me. I got nobody else. You gotta help me figure this out."

"I'm out of options, Hal."

"Tell me what you need. I'll get it."

"Listen, I'm going to shoot straight with you. It's going to be at least a year before the judge is going to reconsider your case."

"A year!"

"Yes. You need to focus on that. You need to stay clean."

"How many times have I gotta say it! I am clean!"

Mr. Wellington stared at me, unmoved. I took a deep breath and looked around the room. Paco was watching me. I turned back to Mr. Wellington. "Sorry," I said.

"It's okay. I understand."

"Well, just don't give up on me. I don't know what I'm

gonna do, but I'm gonna do somethin'. I'm mad as hell about all this."

"I won't give up on you, Hal. But don't make your situation any worse than it already is."

Neither of us spoke for a moment. Finally I stood. "Thanks for comin'," I said.

I went out onto the play yard and crossed to the fence. If the other boys were watching me, I didn't notice. I sat and faced the field, studying the pine trees that Paco wanted to touch. I breathed deep through my nose, trying to pull in the turpentine smell. I just got dirt and asphalt and the sweat of Hellenweiler. Then all of the anger in me was smothered away by a blanket of gloom.

"He's right," I mumbled to myself. "I can't prove anything. Who am I to beat the system?"

I lay back on the ground and let my mind go blank. The sound of crows came across the field.

"They can say whatever they want. They can make me into whatever they want."

The basketballs bounced behind me and the boys yelled. *Was this how it would be for four more years? Me alone in no-man's-land. Maybe I should take Preston up on the offer of leading the Ministers. Maybe I should walk over to Paco and give him the nod and get initiated.* And I saw myself standing among the Hounds, facing Tattoo. He would want to fight me. He would bloody me up and send me to the infirmary. Then I would go to solitary and return days later no different than all the others. A documented violent youth. A piece of trash. The conduct report full, the medical records . . .

Then it came to me. The medical records! I sat up and jerked a look over at Paco. He was watching his boys at their basketball game. "Medical records, Paco," I mumbled aloud. "It's the damn medical records. That's the dirt!"

I kept watching him, but he wouldn't look at me. I faced the fence again and felt my lungs swell with hope.

I wanted desperately to talk to Paco about my new idea, but he was off-limits, surrounded by Hounds. There was only one other person that could help me do anything about it. Fortunately he walked onto the play yard that afternoon.

29

Caboose made for his corner of the fence and took his old position. I stood up and started toward him.

"I'm comin' over," I said. "Like it or not."

He didn't move.

I covered the distance and leaned against the fence next to him and scanned the play yard. The basketballs stopped bouncing on both courts. The Ministers watched. Preston's eyes grew wide and Leroy's mouth hung open. I looked at the Hounds. Paco grinned at me and shook his head. "You see me now, don't you?" I mumbled.

Caboose kept his head low, and no one but me could have seen his mouth moving. "You're lucky you didn't know me before," he said under his breath. "You might not be so sure about this."

"Don't gimme that. I know your game."

"We're not talkin' here."

"Where then? I got an idea and I need your help."

Caboose didn't answer me.

"You don't meet me and I'll follow you around like I'm your best friend until you do."

He scraped the dust with his shoe. "I'll go to the bunk room after supper," he said. "I'll listen to you. But I don't want you to get it in your head that we're any kind of team. I got my own plans. I do things my own way."

"Fine. Just hear me out."

"I told you what I'd do. Now go back down there where you were. This is my corner."

I sat a few chairs down from Caboose during supper. Afterward I went ahead of him to the bunk room while all the other boys went to the rec room. I waited on my bed until he entered and creaked down on his mattress. The floorwalker stepped into the doorway, watched us for a moment, then stepped out.

"Jack told me he had dirt on the guards," I said. "What if we had our own dirt?"

"Jack's got people on the outside. We can't do anything from in here."

"But what if the dirt is already in here?"

Caboose cocked his eyes at me.

"It's got to be the medical records, Caboose. That's got to be what Jack's talkin' about. I'll bet if we could get the medical records we'd have our own dirt."

Caboose looked away again. "Say you could get them. Who would you give 'em to?"

"My lawyer."

"And what makes you think there's anything in there you can use? If you're right and Jack's dad used 'em before, then Mr. Fraley's not gonna let it happen again."

"I don't know. But it's worth a try."

"Not for me. I don't need dirt."

"Yeah? What's gonna happen if you get in trouble with the law after you leave this place? They're gonna pull up your records from Hellenweiler and lock you away for good. You know they're gonna be on you like a cowbird."

"Maybe."

"I need you, Caboose. You know how to get around this place. Maybe there's a way into the infirmary through the basement."

He didn't answer me.

"There is, isn't there? You went out some back way. And you have a key to get down there. You didn't use the one the Ministers had."

No reply.

"Come on, Caboose. What about the infirmary? Can I get in there from the boiler room?"

"Yes. But if you get caught, you might as well move into solitary."

"I gotta try. I can't stand here and do nothin'."

"Yes you can."

"I ain't givin' up."

"Who says anything about givin' up? You just need to be smart. Make them think you gave up."

"So you got a plan?"

"Yeah, I got one," he said. "I'm gonna do my time and walk out that front gate and go straight to a phone book and look up the home address of every guard in this place and kill 'em one by one."

I was about to respond, but my mouth just hung open and the words wouldn't come.

"Kill 'em all for what they did," he said.

"What the hell, Caboose?"

"You can piddle with those medical documents all you want. I don't need any of it."

"Man, they're gonna give you the death sentence."

"They already did that when they killed my brother."

"That's crazy. You gotta stop thinkin' like that."

"You done?"

"No. What if I can get those medical records and there's really somethin' to it all? What if we can get Mr. Fraley in trouble—maybe get him put in jail—would that be good enough?"

"No."

"You killin' everybody doesn't get all the lies off our records. You thought about that? We'll be screwed."

He didn't respond.

"You're just kiddin' me, aren't you?" I said.

"I don't have the key. It's Paco's."

"Man, you and Paco have somethin' goin' on, don't you? I swear there's somethin' between you two."

Caboose didn't say anything for a few seconds. Finally he said, "I can get the key for you, but that's it. You do what you have to do, I'll do what I have to do."

"I'll get it myself. I've got my own weird thing goin' on with Paco. And I know you're not serious about all this killin'."

Caboose got out of his bed and began walking away.

"Thanks," I said after him.

He didn't answer.

30

During supper the next evening, I watched Paco across the room. When I finally caught his eye, I moved my chin slightly in the direction of the confessional. He studied me for a second and looked away.

I waited in the confessional until Paco entered, then I shut the door and put my foot against it.

"How was your stay in solitary?" he said.

"Like a nice vacation."

Paco chuckled. "Good for you."

"Was that your dad I saw you with in the visiting room?" I asked.

"Yes."

"I thought he'd be bigger."

"I take after my mother."

"How often does he come see you?"

"Once a month. It used to be more. He has to drive several hours from Huntsville. But I don't think this meeting is about my father."

"You're right. I saw your other friend Caboose while I was on vacation."

"And he spoke to you?"

"Yeah, he did. You talk to him too, don't you? And you sent him down to the basement, didn't you?"

"It was a contest, my friend. He lost."

"What kind of contest?"

Paco smiled. "You'll have to ask him."

"Whatever, Paco. What is it between you two?"

"We're concerned about our future. I get out right after him. We've discussed business opportunities."

"Yeah, what are you gonna do about him wantin' to kill every guard in this place? You gonna get caught up in that?"

Paco shrugged. "I told you Mr. Fraley walks a thin line. He crossed it a year ago and does not even know it."

"You guys are just gonna go back to jail for the rest of your lives?"

"What else do we know?"

"Man, what's wrong with you? Is this one of your head games again?"

"And surely this meeting is not a lecture."

"I called you here to talk about another way. You and Caboose may be leavin' this place soon, but the rest of us gotta figure somethin' else out."

"Caboose is going to take care of all that for you."

"What good's that gonna do? That still leaves our conduct records that they've messed with."

Paco didn't respond.

"Listen, Paco, there's somethin' you haven't figured out. Sure they're messin' with the conduct reports. But they're messin' with the medical records too. And I think that's the dirt Jack has. My lawyer says if Hellenweiler reports too many injuries the state'll investigate. Then they'd blow this place wide open."

Paco backed against the sink and pushed himself up until he was sitting. "Go on," he said.

"Jack told me it didn't matter how bad he hurt me, no one would know. Which is the truth, right?"

"Mostly. Yes."

"So it all makes sense. Mr. Fraley doesn't want us to get out of here. The only way he can be sure of that is to keep us bad on paper—let the fights happen. But then he has to cover up as many injuries as he can."

Paco studied me without replying.

"Don't you get it?"

"Of course I get it. But how do you prove it?"

"I can't prove the conduct—that's just their word against ours. But I'll tell you how you prove the medical records. When I was in the infirmary the nurse wrote her report and I looked at it. It was all the truth—the whole damn truth on four carbon copies. Then she gave it to Mr. Pratt. It has to change sometime after that. After administration gets it."

"She gave him all four copies?"

"The whole thing. It had a possible concussion on there too. You'd think they'd have to report that."

"So you would have to get a record of what she wrote before it changes?"

"Right. I need your key to the basement. And I need you to show me how to get into the infirmary. That's where it all starts."

"But you would have to wait until someone was hurt."

"Yes. I need to get in right after."

"So we need an initiation?"

"Yeah."

Paco raised his eyebrows. "What does Caboose think about this?"

"He doesn't want anything to do with it."

"Of course not."

"What do you think about it?" I asked.

"I think it's a long shot . . . I'll consider it."

"What do you have to lose?"

Paco rubbed his thick hand over the top of his head. After a moment he said, "I only have a few months left here, Hal. Let's say you get caught. My boys will know I gave you the key."

I wanted to say something, but didn't. Paco watched me and I got the feeling that he read my thoughts anyway.

"But I will consider it," he said.

For several days I watched Paco, waiting for some sign that he wanted to meet. But he seemed to be making an effort to avoid me. Finally toward the end of the week he made his decision. He glanced at me across the mess hall and twitched his chin toward the door.

After supper I went into the confessional. There were already two Ministers talking and using the urinals. They glanced at me and got quiet as I walked behind them. I stood against the wall until they left.

I heard the door open a few minutes later and Paco entered. He pointed to the door and I went behind him and put my foot against it.

"It sure does take you a long time to make a decision," I said.

"Sometimes," he replied, moving toward the sink.

I waited for Paco to continue, but he didn't. He turned on the water and began washing his hands, considering something.

"So what's it gonna be?" I finally said.

"I asked myself why I find friendship with a new boy. And I think, maybe I am still like a new boy myself. Although my body may be bigger, I stopped growing inside myself the day I walked in here. I have learned only how to be a thug. And I will take that away from this place. I will never be a forester. I will never go back to school. It's too late. I am finished."

"Come on, man, you—"

"It is true. I have failed. But you, my friend, have something strong inside that I haven't seen here before. I don't know if it is ignorance, stupidity, or courage, but you have it. And they have not been able to extinguish this thing in you yet, but they will. I don't want to see that happen."

"So you'll help me?"

Paco reached in his pocket and pulled out a key. "Yes," he said. "I'll do what I can. Which is not much. Are you ready?"

"Of course I'm ready. Can't you ever just get to the point?"

31

After we made sure the hall was clear, Paco let me into the utility closet. Once inside, he closed the door and locked it behind us. Then he flipped on the light and we started toward the back.

"My father used to read to me," Paco said as he strolled along.

"Read what?"

"Stories. James Carlos Blake, Gabriel García Márquez, John Steinbeck."

"I never heard of any of those guys."

"That's unfortunate."

"That how you got to be so smart?"

"It is not how smart you are, it is what you learn that matters. Outside of this place I have only made-up stories in my head."

"Why won't you tell me what happened to you?"

"I told you, I don't even remember the truth."

"Like hell."

"I was this boy and then I was someone else."

"Whatever, man."

We turned the corner and started down the corridor to the boiler room stairs. About halfway, Paco stopped and reached above the overhead pipes. His hand came away with a flashlight. He switched it on, saw that it worked, and continued.

We were soon descending the stairs into the strange blue flicker and the breathing and wheezing of machinery. I thought back to the terror of the place the last time I'd seen it. I waited for the fear to grip me, but with Paco I wasn't scared.

We stepped into the water pooled at the base of the stairs. I began to feel the wall for the switch and Paco grabbed my arm. "No," he said. "There are places in this building where you can see the light down here. Remember that."

"Preston turned it on."

"Preston's a fool," he said.

"Yeah, I know."

He flipped on the flashlight. "You must use this. Follow me."

We made our way across the floor, Paco occasionally shining the light back so I could see my way through the machinery and pipes overhead. We traveled deep into the room until the blue flickering was behind us. Finally we came to another set of stairs. Paco turned to me.

"No talking past this point. We are close."

"Can you bust out of Hellenweiler from here?" I asked.

"No. But these stairs will lead you into another utility corridor similar to the one you saw before. Open the door at the end of it and you will be three steps from the infirmary. To your right will be the offices and the visiting room. As you know, there is another set of locked doors beyond that."

"Why don't you just get a key to those too?"

"I should tell you the story of the keys sometime."

"Sure. I guess whenever you decide to tell me about how you got sent to Hellenweiler."

Paco got the key from his pocket and gave it to me. "You have what you need now. If you get caught, the guards will finish you off in solitary. Your first stay was easy. A week in there will suck you dry of any spirit you have left. There will be no more hope for you."

"Thanks for the encouragement."

Paco turned to go. "It's only truth. Let's get out of here before we're missed."

All I needed was another initiation. I was sure my plan would work. It had to work. It was all I had left.

Every time I stepped into the bunk room, I studied the bunks in no-man's-land to see if they'd been recently made. But the days slipped by without any sign of a new boy. I went about my routine—breakfast, school, lunch, school again, play yard, bunk room. No one talked to me, no one watched me. Occasionally I glanced at Paco and Caboose, and even though they ignored me, I let myself believe they were my friends, acting out their own strange games of survival in this place.

The blue skies and heat of an Alabama summer were starting to burn away the cool spring weather. The play yard became dry and dusty and smelled of burnt rubber. I sat with my face against the fence, watching meadowlarks in the field, no longer concerned with what was behind me. Sometimes a man on a tractor would pull a disk across the field to kill any young sprouts that tried to grow there. The dirt was always kept bare and loose, waiting to record the footprints of anyone that tried to cross it.

One afternoon I studied the far trees where frenzied

blackbirds flocked in the top of a giant live oak. I didn't have long before the buzzer called us in to supper. There was no way to tell time, but I'd developed a strange sick feeling that rose in my chest—some kind of internal clock that anticipated that awful sound.

I saw a car moving slowly in and out of shadow along the turn row at the far end of the field. The car looked familiar, but I couldn't place it. When it approached the live oak, the blackbirds lifted from the tree. I watched them until the last one disappeared into the depths of the forest. Then their calls were lost to me and I returned my focus to the car. It parked under the shade of the oak. After a moment I heard two doors slam.

"Hey, Hal!" someone shouted.

I sat up straight and strained my eyes. Carla took a step into the field and waved at me. My heart leaped and I stood and clenched the wire with my hands. I looked over at Caboose. He was turned and watching.

Carla's older sister, Rhonda, stepped up behind her.

"Your daddy said to tell you he misses you!" Carla yelled.

I squeezed the wire. She looked so good and fresh it made me want to cry.

"I'll be waitin' for you!" she yelled.

A Hellenweiler maintenance truck was coming up fast behind them. Rhonda gave Carla a tug on the arm, but she didn't move. I felt a knot swelling in my throat.

"I miss you too!" I yelled.

She blew me a kiss. "Don't do that," I mumbled.

The truck stopped and a guard got out.

"Thanks for comin'!" I yelled.

The guard said something to Rhonda and gestured angrily for them to leave. I waved helplessly as Rhonda tugged at Carla's arm. Then I felt someone grab my shoulder and spin me around. Mr. Pratt shoved me away from the fence so hard I almost lost my balance.

"What in hell you think you're doin'!" he yelled.

I tried to get one last look across the field, but he shoved me toward the building again. "Get inside! You pull that again and you'll be in solitary for a week!"

I started across the play yard just as the buzzer sounded. I smiled. I'd trade a week in solitary any day to see her again.

32

A week passed with no sign of a new boy. I kept watch over the field, hoping that somehow Carla would come back, but I knew it wouldn't happen.

That evening I lay on my bunk after supper. I heard someone enter and looked over to see Caboose. He lumbered down the aisle and settled into his bed.

"What are you doin' in here?" I asked.

"Paco's actin' strange," he said.

I glanced across the aisle at him. He stared at the underside of the mattress above him. "What's wrong with him?" I asked.

"I don't know. I thought maybe he would've told you."

"No. He hardly talks to me anymore."

"Me neither," Caboose said.

"I don't get when the two of you would talk anyway. I never see you together."

"The boiler room."

"That makes sense," I said.

"I get out in eight days."

I took a deep breath and let it out. "That your eighteenth birthday?"

"Yeah."

"You still serious about what you wanna do?"

"Yeah."

"I wish you hadn't told me all that. Maybe you should talk to your daddy or somebody first."

Caboose made a grunting sound that was about as close as he came to a laugh. "Dad? There's nobody left. They all moved away."

"Where you gonna go?"

"Grandaddy left me and my brother his old salvage yard full of cars before he died. There's a little house on it. We were always gonna fix it up."

"Where is it?"

"Outside a town called Clinton."

"I know where that place is! I used to go by there and get parts for our truck. That's crazy!"

Caboose didn't seem surprised.

"There's still tons of cars," I said. "Cars and trucks and just about everything."

"I stole cars," he said. "You could hide 'em easy in that place. My little brother just wanted to be like me."

I heard someone enter the room and glanced over to see the floorwalker. He studied us for a moment and then stepped out again.

"I have this weird thought sometimes," I said. "It's kind of good and bad. Maybe after people die they can really know what you think. Like it's really hard for me to tell my daddy that I love him, but I think one day after he's gone, he'll be able to know my thoughts. But he's also gonna know about all the bad stuff I did too . . . But that's fine. I just want him to hear me think about him."

"I want my brother to know I got revenge for him."

"I don't think he'd want it. What good's it gonna do him?"

Caboose didn't answer me.

"And what good's it gonna do you? It ain't gonna make you feel any better. And I still don't see how Paco fits into any of that. He ain't gonna hang out with a killer."

"I can't believe I'm layin' here talkin' to you," he said.

"I'm glad you did. I'm lonely as hell, Caboose. I gotta get out of here. You saw that girl, didn't you?"

"Yeah, I saw her."

"Curled your toes up, didn't she?"

"I don't know about that."

"She's fine, is what she is. You think I can keep from jumpin' that fence with somebody like that out there? Hell."

"How's the plan comin'?"

"I just need an initiation. I need somebody to go to the infirmary. Then I'm gonna see about those records."

Caboose sighed. "Don't get your hopes up."

Daddy always told me that bad luck came in threes. But at Hellenweiler it never stopped.

On Thursday, Leroy stepped up behind me in the lunch line. I was eating late and he was coming for seconds. "Jack's back," he said over my shoulder. The words hit me like a fist to my gut. I nodded slowly without turning around.

"I saw him walk into Mr. Fraley's office a few minutes ago."

"All right," I said.

"Watch out, Hal."

"Thanks."

I got my food and took it to no-man's-land. I sat next to Caboose.

"Looks like I'll be the next person in the infirmary," I said.

Caboose didn't look at me. "What are you talkin' about?" he said.

"Jack's back."

He stopped chewing and turned to look at the Ministers' table.

"He's not in here yet," I said. "Leroy saw him go into Mr. Fraley's office."

Caboose turned back to his food. "Don't go into the confessional," he said. "If he comes toward you in the yard, come stand next to me."

"How about I stand with you all the time?"

"We're not a gang."

"Man, you're gonna be out of here in a week."

"And let's hope you get an initiation before I leave."

"I guess I'm just gonna have to fight him on the play yard. That's all there is to it. I'm gonna have to get it over with and move on. He can't hurt me too bad out there. I might even get in a few good punches before he cleans my clock."

"You'd be better off joinin' up with Paco before that happens."

I took a bite of food and considered it. After a few seconds of working all the angles, I realized he was right. Strategically, joining Paco's gang would be my best move. But there were so many pieces to the twisted game that my mind was getting tangled.

"You got me covered for a week, right?"

"I'll do what I can," he said.

"Good. I'll see you on the yard after class."

"You don't seem very worried."

"I've already fought Jack in my head so much I figure I'm ready."

33

I waited on the yard, watching the admin door. I was surprised when Paco casually stepped away from the Hounds and started toward me. The basketballs went silent on both ends of the court and all eyes were upon him. He stopped next to me and slid down the fence to sit like the time when we were generals.

"Things didn't quite work out like you thought, did they?"

I sat down next to him. "What are you doin', man? The whole yard's lookin' at you."

"Yes, well."

"Well, what?"

"First of all, I want to tell you about the story of the keys. It is really a very simple story."

"The keys?"

"Yes. You see—"

"I don't care about the damn keys. Jack's about to stroll out here to kick my ass and I gotta get next to Caboose."

Paco held a finger up for silence. "You see, Jack blackmailed a guard for two sets about six months ago. He can get those kinds of things. It was his idea that both gangs would have a private place to settle disputes one-on-one."

"Great. Now I know about the keys. Are we done with your story of the day?"

"No. There is one more. My father is a rocket scientist for NASA. I had—"

"A rocket scientist!"

"Yes, I had—"

"That's crazy!"

He looked over the play yard again. "I had a nice brick house in an upscale neighborhood. I had a mother who loved me and a young sister who is very pretty. I went to the best school in Huntsville. I was captain of the chess team and held the number two spot on the scholars' bowl team. But you know what?"

I shook my head.

"I could not walk into a classroom without someone calling me a name or throwing something at me. They called me the stump. They called me the grease face. And I sat in the back row and said nothing while they whispered and looked at me and laughed. In the halls they thumped the back of my head and taped notes to my shirt. I said nothing. I did nothing. They stole my clothes during PE and I said nothing and did nothing. I never understood why these things were done to me. I was ashamed to talk to my parents about it. I had no friends to talk to."

I didn't know what to say.

"For a while, I was able to block the comments out so that they existed like static around me. I could sit at my desk and listen to the teacher through the static. My body became nothing more than a wrapper for one who lives totally in his mind. The thumps and prods fell on this soft wrapper without my feeling anything. I was still alive deep inside my head. And it was like that for a while. And I thought that was how it was going to be. It was just my brain and what it absorbed through the static. But one day I began to hear a tiny, distant ringing noise. Like a mosquito. And this mosquito got louder and louder. Then it separated into strands of noise and became the jeers and mumbling and ridicule of the students, only an amplified, torturous version of it. I felt their pokes and prods magnified, like my skin had grown supersensitive."

Paco paused and looked across the field and drew a deep breath through his nose. Then he let out the breath and left his eyes on the far trees.

"I snapped," he finally said. "I began picking up desks and throwing them at students from the back of the room. They screamed and ran for the door. They tried to get out, but they couldn't all fit through. All I had to do was throw the desks at the cluster of them."

"Christ, Paco."

"I hurt a lot of kids that day."

I heard the admin door slam. I glanced up and saw Jack looking over the play yard. Mr. Pratt was gone.

"I'm about to have to stand up, Paco."

"Give me a moment, my friend."

Jack rested his eyes on me and studied the strange scene of me and Paco against the fence. Then he turned and walked over to the Ministers. Preston backed away while the others went to meet him.

"I don't know if I have a moment," I said.

"You see," Paco continued, "I began as an acne-faced egghead. Who would know a kid like me had the potential to be such a violent youth? But it was there. It is in all of us when you strip away dignity and hope. I brought that rage with me to Hellenweiler. And I used it again on the boy I beat with a rock."

I listened to Paco while Jack talked to Preston and the rest of the Ministers.

"Paco?"

"I could have been a forester."

The Ministers were all turned, looking at me.

"Paco?"

"Instead, I am this. I will always be this."

Jack began walking toward me, the rest of the Ministers following.

"I gotta go, Paco."

Paco nodded slowly and I began to stand. Suddenly he grabbed my arm and held me. "No, you stay here today, my friend. I'll see you tonight."

"What?"

But he pulled me down and stood in my place. Jack was almost to us and Paco took a step toward him and stopped. They were faced off, Jack's cheeks twitching and the fire dancing in his eyes.

"Get out of my way," Jack said.

Caboose had moved toward us a few steps and watched intently. Jack stared at Paco and pointed to Caboose at the same time. "I want both of you to stay out of this," Jack said.

Paco didn't respond.

"Hal's not even a Hound!" Jack said. "He's nothin'! He's in no-man's-land!"

"So am I," said Paco.

Caboose took another step but Paco stopped him. "You heard him, Caboose. Stay out of it."

Jack's hands fidgeted at his sides.

"Hit me," Paco said.

"What? I don't have anything against you."

Now the Hounds were drifting over. Paco looked across Jack's shoulder at the rest of the Ministers. He raised his voice just loud enough for them to hear. "I'm asking you to hit me, coward."

Jack started to turn and look back at his gang, but stopped and faced Paco again. The fire in his eyes was dimmer and something had gone slack about his face.

"Hey, Paco!" Tattoo yelled. "What's goin' on? This isn't a Hound fight."

Preston had moved to the front of the Ministers. "Hit him, Paco," Preston said.

I studied Preston in disbelief. He looked at me, his eyes dancing with excitement and an idiot grin spreading across his face. I shook my head at his stupidity.

"Fight me or your friends behind you, Jack," Paco said. "Looks like Preston's already in line for your spot."

Jack was cornered. The tension jerked into his face again and I could almost hear the angry hornets. He charged and rammed Paco against the fence. I rolled out of the way and got to my knees and watched. Jack began driving his fists into Paco's kidneys over and over while Paco did nothing to defend himself. Slowly, Paco began to double over until he was on his knees. Jack backed off, surprised at himself. Caboose took another step forward, but somehow Paco saw this and signaled for him to stand back. Jack came at

Paco again and began hammering his face with the fury of an insane person. Paco's big head went right and left with the blows, his eyes open the whole time, watching, waiting, while he did nothing. The Ministers cheered and the Hounds were a silent huddle behind them. I saw Caboose's giant legs beside me, but I couldn't take my eyes off the fight. I couldn't believe the beating Paco was taking. Then he finally rolled over onto his side. Jack began cursing him and kicking him in the ribs. Paco doubled up and coughed blood onto the dirt. Suddenly Mr. Pratt was grabbing Jack and pulling him away.

"That's enough, Jack!"

"You see who's the man!" Jack yelled. "You feel that! Call me a coward!"

Jack struggled against Mr. Pratt and managed to turn and face the Ministers. "You all see that! Don't ever get in my face!"

Mr. Pratt squeezed Jack to his chest and drug him backward. "I'm gonna have to take you to solitary for this, Jack."

"The hell you are!"

"We'll talk to Mr. Fraley about it."

"Yeah, we will! Let's go see him!" Jack let out a crazy laugh. "Then I'll see every one of you at dinner tonight!"

I crawled over to Paco. Caboose stepped past me and bent down and picked him up and put him over his shoulder like he weighed nothing. Blood drooled out of his mouth and down Caboose's back. I stood, wanting to help, but there was nothing I could do.

The Ministers and Hounds parted and let Mr. Pratt and Jack through. Caboose followed behind with Paco.

Before they made it halfway across the yard, another guard met them and motioned for Caboose to put Paco down. Caboose ignored him and kept walking. The guard started to say something but didn't. Soon they disappeared through the administration door.

I fixed my eyes on Preston. He looked like he'd swallowed poison.

34

Jack was not at supper. Caboose came in late, got his food, and sat next to me.

"This better work," he mumbled.

I looked at the Hound table. Tattoo was eyeing us. "I know," I said. "I'm goin' to the infirmary right after we eat."

"What do you need me to do?" he said.

"Watch my back until you have to leave."

"Yours and Paco's now."

"How bad is he hurt?" I asked.

"Bad enough."

"Jack's not here," I said.

"He's prob'ly sleepin' in Mr. Fraley's guest bedroom."

"Are you serious?"

Caboose cocked his eyes at me and didn't answer.

I slipped into the utility corridor just after supper. I flipped on the light and hurried toward the boiler room. I stopped long enough to grab the flashlight from its hiding place, then continued to the stairs.

The room was more sinister than ever when I faced it alone in the darkness with the throbbing machines in my ears. I desperately wanted to turn on the lights, but remembered what Paco had told me. I shined the flashlight beam through the blue flicker and pressed forward.

I finally came to the stairs and took them two at a time, eager to leave the boiler room behind. Soon I was walking the corridor and then I was at the door. I pressed my ear to it and heard nothing. Most of the guards were gone for the day. Only the floorwalker and the rec room guard would still be on duty. My only problem was the nurse. I hoped she wasn't around.

I cracked the door and looked out. The hall was empty. I set the flashlight down and found a slip of paper on the floor. I stepped out into the hall and shut the door behind me, placing the paper in the lock so that it wouldn't engage.

Three steps and I was able to peer into the window glass of the infirmary. I saw Paco lying in bed with bandages on his face and wrapped around his torso. He seemed to be sleeping. Otherwise, the room was empty. I opened the door and slipped in.

The clipboard hung on the wall beside the bed and I reached up and pulled it down.

"Hey, friend," Paco croaked.

I jumped at his voice and almost dropped the clipboard. "Damnit, Paco! You wanna give me a heart attack?"

He tried to smile but jerked at the pain of it. "Do you have what you need?"

I looked down at the report. It was almost a full page of writing. "It looks like it. You gonna make it?"

"Don't worry about me. I'll be all right. Make sure they put broken ribs on there."

I nodded.

"You did good," he said.

"The hell. I'm gonna get Caboose to kick your ass over what you pulled."

Paco's eyes grew wide with humor. "Get out of here," he finally said.

I tore the last carbon from the report and replaced the clipboard on the wall. I folded the paper and crammed it in my pocket. Then I nodded at Paco and he blinked his eyes slowly.

I retraced my route back through the boiler room, up the cement steps at the other side, and through the utility corridor. I paused at the door and listened. The boys were in the rec room. The hall was silent. I opened the door, slipped out, and eased my back against it until the lock clicked. I hadn't taken two steps before I heard a voice behind me.

"Where have you been?"

I spun around, my heart racing and blood rushing to my ears. There was Mr. Pratt. I didn't know what he'd seen.

"I asked you a question," he said.

"I was in the bunk room."

"I just came from there, smart-ass. Where have you been?"

"I mean, I was in the bunk room and then I had to use the restroom."

"Why didn't you use the one in there?"

I swallowed. "I don't know. I just didn't . . . I like the washroom better."

He studied me for what seemed like a long time. Then he glanced at the shirt pocket on my jumpsuit. I could feel the folded bulk of the report standing out against my chest.

"What you got in there?" he said.

"A letter."

By the way he studied it, you would think he was reading through the fabric. "You really think writin' to her is gonna do any good?" he finally said.

I took a deep breath. "Nossir."

He looked me in the eyes again. "You're right. Now, get in your rack or go in the rec room with the other boys. You don't just roam around here like you own the place."

"Yessir," I said.

I got back to the bunk room just in time to write my letter to Daddy.

> *Dear Daddy,*
>   *Get this to Mr. Wellington. This is very important. Tell him to get the copies of this report from the people at Hellenweiler. He will know what to do. Both of you have to trust me one last time.*
>
>   *Love,*
>   *Hal*

I stuffed the letter and the report into the envelope, addressed it, stamped it, and stuck it in my locker. Not a moment later, the boys started filing in. Caboose walked up and studied me. I nodded to him and he turned away and began getting undressed for showers. Then Preston walked past with a towel over his shoulder. He stopped and turned back to me like he had something to say. But Caboose was already there, looking down at him. Preston swallowed and left.

I took my place next to Caboose at breakfast Friday morning. I faced the Ministers' table and saw that Jack was still missing. His boys were rowdy and back to their old selves. Except for Preston. Worries weighed heavily on his mind and I could see him shrinking back into the wuss he used to be.

A note was passed to me in the classroom.

> *Hal, I need to talk to you. In private. Meet me in*
> *the confessional tonight.*
> *Preston*

I turned around in my desk and looked at him. Suddenly, he was the same pathetic whiner I knew back at Pinson. His eyes had gone soft and his face had the slack of a person living in dread of something awful about to come down on him.

I crumpled the paper and let him watch it fall to the floor.

That afternoon I waited for Caboose outside my classroom. It wasn't long before the older boys were dismissed and he lumbered past. He twitched his finger for me to follow and I fell in behind him. When we walked onto the play yard Tattoo and the Hounds eyed us curiously from their court. But I wasn't worried about them. They would leave me alone until they got through with Paco. The Ministers were what I was concerned about. They wanted me. I doubted they would try anything until Jack came on the yard, but I was sticking close to Caboose just in case.

Caboose and I took our stand in his usual corner of the fence.

"Who would you bet on between Tattoo and Paco?" I said.

"Tattoo."

"Why didn't Tattoo fight him before now?"

"Paco intimidated him. But now he's gone soft. And Tattoo knows it. And Tattoo is meaner."

"So it's over for him with the Hounds, no matter what?"

"Yes. Both of you are against this fence from now on."

"I'm gonna send the letter as soon as he gets out of the infirmary. We've got to make sure the nurse has given the clipboard to Mr. Pratt. They have to have time to change it or get rid of it or whatever they do. If my lawyer calls too soon, we're busted."

"Don't screw this up."

"I ain't screwin' it up. And we're all gonna get through this. And you ain't gonna do all that revenge you been goin' on about. They'll get what's comin' to 'em."

Caboose scratched the dirt with his toe and didn't answer me.

"You and Paco can start a lawn service or somethin'."

"What are you talkin' about?"

"Man, you can make some good money at that. My daddy did it for a while. Paco likes trees and stuff."

Caboose spit at the ground and rubbed it into the dust with his shoe. "I got nothin' waitin' on me. A whole lot of nothin'."

"What happened to your parents?"

"I don't know."

"Don't know or don't wanna talk about it?"

"Just because Paco likes to sit and spout off his mumbo jumbo don't mean I do. I've been in here plenty long enough to think about what I want when I leave, and some wet-behind-the-ears new boy ain't gonna make me rethink it."

"Fine. But you still stuck your neck out for me down in the boiler room with Jack."

"Don't let it go to your head. I lost the coin toss."

I sighed and slid down the fence to sit. "All right. I'll shut up . . . Coin toss my butt."

Caboose looked at me. "Did he tell you?"

"No, but it wasn't no coin toss. I know that much."

35

When Caboose and I entered the mess hall for supper, the Ministers' table was frenzied. Jack was holding court. Then I noticed Preston sitting alone in no-man's-land. He picked at his food and kept his head down. Someone from the Ministers' table threw a dinner roll and it bounced off his shoulder.

"We got company," I told Caboose. He glanced at Preston and continued on through the food line.

We took our seats a few chairs down from Preston and began to eat. I glanced at the Ministers and saw Jack staring at me. He slid his finger across his throat.

"Jack doesn't look like he lost much attitude in solitary," I said.

Caboose didn't answer me.

"You really think they let him stay somewhere else?"

Caboose nodded slightly.

"What are we gonna do about Preston?"

"Let him get what's comin'," he mumbled.

I looked over at Preston. He kept his head down. Finally I sighed. "Come on down here if you want," I said to him.

He hesitated for a moment, then picked up his tray and came to sit next to me. Caboose frowned.

"Thanks," Preston said.

"Don't thank me yet," I said. "I haven't made up my mind about you. Where's Paco?"

"I don't know."

"Yeah you do. You got your nose in everybody's business."

Preston looked at the Ministers and swallowed nervously. "He went to solitary this afternoon."

Caboose and I exchanged a look.

"You wanna be with us, Preston?"

"Yeah," he said.

"Okay. But we got our own initiation."

"What is it?"

"I don't know yet. I'll be thinkin' about it. You better talk to somebody about transferrin' to Chase's old bed."

Preston gathered his bedding and personal items from the Ministers' end of the bunk room after supper while Caboose lay on his bed and I sat on the floor beside him.

"I ain't watchin' out for him," Caboose said.

"Don't then. He's no worse off for it."

"You're soft."

"You are too, you just forgot."

Caboose didn't say anything.

"I'll put that letter in the outgoin' mail first thing in the mornin'."

That night I lay in my bunk listening for noises coming from seg. But I knew Paco wouldn't utter a word. He was too strong. He'd lie there and die before he gave the guards any satisfaction.

"I'm sorry for everything, Hal," Preston whispered.

"You're scared. You're not sorry."

"Quiet down there!" yelled the floorwalker.

Saturday morning the three of us went to breakfast together. In the hall was the basket for outgoing mail and I dropped the letter into it as we passed. It would normally take a day to get to Daddy, but mail didn't run on Sunday so it might take two this time. Caboose would leave on Thursday. After that, Preston and I would be on our own and the Ministers would close in on us. There would be no help from Paco even if he got out of solitary. He had his own problems. Now that he had betrayed the Hounds, Tattoo and the rest of the dogs were waiting to punish him.

"What's your plan, Hal?"

"Shut up, Preston."

Caboose let Preston and me stay next to him on the play yard. He stood the entire time while we sat on either side of his big legs. I tried to get him to talk, but he was somewhere far away in his head. If I asked him a question, sometimes he'd give me a short reply. Sometimes he wouldn't answer at all. Preston knew he wasn't invited to talk.

"I'm gonna race cars one day, Caboose. Race on a dirt track. Even if I have to wait until I'm eighteen. You ever been to a dirt track?"

No answer.

"Man, it's so loud you can feel the engines through

180

your butt. You know, they slide around the turns. It's not like asphalt. And they don't have windshields. Get mud all over their face . . . I know I'd be good at it. I used to drive our truck around the clay pit, and I mean hammer-down drivin'. I could throw dirt fifty feet in third gear. Yeah, I could show them dirt racers. Don't you have somethin' you know you'd be good at?"

No answer.

"I dream about car engines and greasy nuts and bolts. Every time I think about jammin' my foot down on a gas pedal it makes me grind my teeth together."

"I've been to a dirt-track race before," Preston said.

"Shut up, Preston . . . I'm tellin' you, Caboose. I can rub my fingers together and feel the grease. It's in me . . . You can make money doin' it too. Imagine if that was your job—racin'. Man, what do you think about that?"

Caboose moved his foot a little bit.

"But I bet you couldn't fit in one of those cars. You go in through the window. They weld the doors shut."

"I gotta pee," Preston said.

"Shut up, Preston. Go pee if you have to."

He looked away and didn't move.

The days slipped by with no word from the outside and my spirit sank lower and lower with each passing hour. By Wednesday I admitted to myself I'd been foolish to think that I could start a crackdown on an entire boys' home with one simple piece of paper. Even if it was enough, from what I'd seen, it took weeks to get Judge Mackin to consider anything. And there I was out of ideas and out of time, facing my nightmares. My fight with Jack was coming. My fight with him and my future of being an outcast in no-man's-land. Fence meat for the Ministers and the Hounds. Me and Paco and Preston.

"They're all talkin', Hal. Both sides."

"I know, Leroy. You gotta get over it and stop comin' up to me like this."

"Caboose is gone tomorrow."

"You think I don't know that? You wanna be on the fence with us? Get out of here."

I lay down in my rack and closed my eyes. I thought about Carla. *She was crazy to ever be your girlfriend*, I mumbled.

That last night we were together, after I kissed her on the tailgate, she told me she didn't care that I was going to juve. I didn't see how that could be. Not for a girl like her.

"I figured you wouldn't wanna have anything else to do with me," I told her.

She shook her head, no.

"How come you still like me?" I asked.

"Because you're the only boy I know that isn't trying to be like everybody else."

"Maybe that's what got me in all this trouble. Shoot, I don't even know how regular boys act anymore."

"Well, that's what I like. And I think you're stronger than any boys I know at school."

I puffed up a little. "You think?"

She nodded and leaned against me. "In lots of ways."

* * *

I was lying in bed with my eyes open when Mr. Pratt turned on the light Thursday morning. I listened to the boys groan and complain and climb off their bunks. I looked over at Preston and his face was pale as a bedsheet.

Mr. Pratt came walking down the aisle, shaking the bunks of people that were slow to rise.

"Ten minutes to breakfast," he said.

I sat up and studied Caboose. He lay with his hands behind his head, staring at the underside of the bunk above him. Soon Mr. Pratt was standing before us. He tossed a plastic grocery bag at him. "Strip your sheets," he said. "Put your personal items in the bag and report to Mr. Fraley's office for checkout."

Caboose sat up slowly and picked the bag off his stomach. Mr. Pratt continued down the aisle. I slid off my bunk and stood there with Preston while Caboose began removing his sheets.

"Happy birthday," I said.

Caboose didn't respond.

"They don't give you much of a goin'-away party, do they?"

"Hal?" Preston said.

"Just make up your bed, Preston. I don't have any answers for you."

Preston began to make his bed and I did the same. We both took our time, waiting for the other boys to leave. Before long, we were the only three left in the room. Preston leaned on his bedpost and waited quietly. Caboose picked through his locker and dropped a few things into the bag.

"What are you two waitin' on?" he mumbled. "I'm not headed your way this time."

"What are you gonna do?" I asked him.

"I'm goin' to the junkyard."

"You think they'll just let you walk out of here?"

"It looks like it."

"Then what?"

Caboose came away from the locker and stood and looked at me. "Your way didn't work, Hal. Now it's time for my way."

"What's he talkin' about?" Preston said.

"Shut up, Preston . . . Caboose, you—"

"It's too late," he said. "It's too late for all of us."

"Go see my daddy. At least go see him and tell him what's happenin' here. Let him know that I did my best."

Caboose studied me.

"Just do that for me. It's not even far from your house. Talk to him about what you're gonna do."

Caboose shook his head doubtfully and turned to go. Preston and I followed.

"Don't then," I said. "Just go see him."

"Tell Paco I'll be waitin' for him," Caboose said over his shoulder.

"Yeah, in the state pen."

Caboose walked out the door into the hall. My mind searched desperately for something else to say to him.

"Caboose," I said.

He didn't slow. I came to the mess room and stopped and watched him continue down the hall. He passed through the double doors and on toward Mr. Fraley's office.

I took a deep breath and let it out. Then I turned to Preston.

"You ready to go in there?" I asked him.

"We're dead."

"Yeah, well don't be a wuss about it. Come on."

36

Paco was back. I studied him sitting alone in no-man's-land and I could see that he was in no condition to help us or himself. His face was still swollen and he could barely keep his head up over the food tray.

Preston and I got our breakfast and sat across from him. "You all right?" I asked him.

"Yes."

Paco glanced at Preston. "What's he doing here?"

"He bet on the wrong guy."

Paco nodded. "That makes twice for you, Preston."

Preston picked at his food in silence.

"I was hoping you would have everything worked out by the time I saw you again," Paco said.

"We're still waitin'. Caboose left this mornin'."

"I know," Paco said.

Suddenly a biscuit came flying over the table and hit Paco in the forehead and fell onto his tray. "Traitor!" a Hound yelled.

Paco calmly picked up the biscuit and set it aside. "We'll take the fence," he said. "We'll deal with whatever they bring us."

"You look like you're about to pass out."

He didn't answer.

"I wish you could have talked to Caboose before he

left," I said. "He won't listen to me. He's still set on his big plan."

"He's carried that with him for a long time."

"I tried to talk him out of it."

A wadded-up wet napkin came over our table and hit me in the shoulder. I looked at the Ministers' table and they were watching me and laughing.

I turned to Preston. "Who you think Jack wants more, me or you?"

"You," he said.

"That's what I figure."

The boys were unusually quiet in class that day, like they all had a secret. Preston sat beside me, and whenever I looked over at him, he returned my stare. Something in his eyes pleaded for an answer. But I didn't have answers. Once, I turned around and looked at Leroy in the back corner. He had his head down on the desk and wouldn't face me.

During lunch the three of us ate silently. It was almost time to go when Paco finally spoke.

"Wait by your classroom door after school today. I'll come get you. Then we walk straight to the fence. Understand?"

Preston and I nodded as the buzzer went off.

We waited for Paco after class. Then the three of us hung back while the other boys filed past onto the yard. Paco leaned against the wall and held his hand to his ribs and winced.

"You can't go out there," I said.

"We don't have a choice."

"What if we just go inside and tell 'em we ain't goin'."

"Then it will be tomorrow. Or the next day. It doesn't matter."

Preston's hands were shaking.

"You better buck up, Preston. I ain't takin' your beatin' for you."

"I can't fight, Hal. You know that."

"Yeah, I know. But you better get mean out there. I mean pit bull mean."

Paco came away from the wall. "Remember, straight to the fence, then turn around and face them. Always keep your back to the fence. Only one at a time can come at you that way. I will stand on the side of the Ministers and you two will be on the side of the Hounds. They will have to cross up to get at us. The more of them we get fighting each other, the fewer there will be to concentrate on us."

"Preston," I said, "you stay in the middle, since they're comin' for me first."

Preston swallowed and studied his feet.

"Forget about your initiation," I said. "I figure this'll do for it."

Preston nodded.

Paco took a step toward the yard. "Let's go," he said.

The basketballs were not moving that day. Both sides of the yard were as silent as a church, the boys watching us arrive and make our way to the fence. We made it halfway before Mr. Pratt turned and stepped inside.

"There he goes," I mumbled.

"Don't stop," Paco said. "Get to the fence."

The Hounds and Ministers were already coming away from their courts and closing in behind us. Tattoo and Jack walked out in front of the two gangs. We kept moving, Paco leading the way, then Preston, and finally me.

We reached the fence and turned one by one and put our backs to the wire in the order we'd discussed. I didn't focus on Jack or any of the boys in particular. The whole mass of them drifted toward us as one. I focused somewhere beyond them so that they all blurred together.

"Helpless Hal!" one of the blurred shapes said.

They were stopped now, the Ministers and the Hounds all crossed and mingled together like Paco had said. Jack slowly came into focus before me. He was no more than two feet away, his face electric with tension. He wanted to rip me to pieces. And it wasn't something he was doing to impress anyone. He wanted the feel of it and he had a good excuse. I glanced at Tattoo beside him. He was eye-balling Paco, ready to claim his title as leader of the Hounds.

"Who's gonna step in for you now, Helpless?" Jack said to me.

I didn't answer him.

"I always knew you were weak," Tattoo said to Paco.

"You hit us, you hit yourselves," Paco said. "You only perpetuate the foolishness. But the two of you will never know this. There is no hope for you."

I let my eyes focus on Jack. I felt anger rising in me

189

and I clenched my teeth against it. "I never asked anybody to step in for me the first time," I said. "I ain't askin' now."

Jack took a step even closer.

"Bring it on," I said. "Let's do it right this time."

37

Like Paco said, the dogs preyed on fear, and now I had none. Something in Jack's expression changed the slightest bit when he saw how committed I was to fighting him. For several seconds we stared at each other and I detected a twitch of indecision in his eyes. But there was also something else happening. In my periphery I heard and saw flashes of cars going by outside the fence. Had I not been eye-locked with Jack, I would have turned and looked with the other boys.

"The cops are here," somebody said.

I still didn't look. Jack's eyes darted toward the parking lot then came back to me.

"I'm right here," I said to him.

"A bunch of 'em," somebody else said.

Suddenly the administration door flew open and slammed against the wall. It was violent enough to make Jack turn around. Mr. Pratt was rushing toward us like something had scared him out of the building.

"Back off!" he yelled from across the yard.

The boys began moving to get out of his way.

"Everybody, faces against the fence. Now!"

The boys began to shuffle to the fence on either side of us. Only Jack and I remained where we were.

Then Jack took a step toward Mr. Pratt. "Your break ain't up yet," he said.

But Mr. Pratt kept coming until they were nose to nose. A strange, worried look pulled at the guard's face and his nostrils flared as he breathed heavily through them.

"Maybe I should get Daddy to remind you of a few things," Jack said.

Mr. Pratt grabbed Jack by the shirt and lifted him and plunged him into the fence. Before Jack could react, the guard spun him around and used one palm to press his face into the wire mesh. "Shut your mouth and do what I say!" he said. Then he turned to me. *"Get your face against the fence!"*

I quickly did as he said. During the shuffle, Paco had somehow ended up next to me. He had his nose to the wire and I stared at the side of his face. "You see the trees, my friend?" he said quietly.

Jack grunted as Mr. Pratt pressed him harder.

"Something's going down inside," Paco said. "Something big."

Paco barely got the words from his mouth before I heard more adult voices behind us.

"Guard! Step away from the boy!" someone shouted. It was a familiar voice, but I couldn't place it.

"There was about to be a fight out here!" Mr. Pratt yelled over his shoulder.

"Get away from the boy!" came the voice again.

I heard the fence crink as Mr. Pratt's hand let up. There were footsteps everywhere in the yard behind us.

"I want all of you boys to take one step back, turn around, and sit," the voice said.

When I turned, Officer Pete was leading four police officers in our direction. I went to my knees and began shaking my head. Then I felt a lump rise in my throat and I coughed against it. "Paco," I said.

"I see them," he replied. "Sit down."

I felt like the weight had dropped out of me and I sat back in the puddle of it. "Get me out of this damn place."

"Patience," Paco said.

I saw Mr. Wellington step onto the play yard and start toward us. I locked eyes with him until Mr. Pratt yelled out, "What's goin' on here?"

"Where's Fraley?" Officer Pete asked him.

"In his office, I guess! What's all this about?"

Another policeman came through the administration door followed by a red-faced Mr. Fraley. "I found him, Pete!" the policeman called out.

Mr. Fraley stomped up next to Mr. Pratt and turned to face Officer Pete. "What's the meaning of this?" he demanded.

"Is this how you control your boys?" Officer Pete said.

"I asked you a question!" Mr. Fraley replied.

Officer Pete stepped up close and towered over him so that they almost touched, chin to nose. "You better cool that attitude, podna."

Mr. Fraley opened his mouth and started to reply, but didn't. Then his jowls began to quiver like Jell-O. Officer Pete stayed there a moment longer, letting his message sink in before he took a step back. "Come up here, Wellington," he finally said. "Hand me that medical report."

Mr. Wellington came forward with a folder in one hand. He pulled a sheet of paper from it and gave it to Officer Pete. I recognized the injury report I'd sent him.

Officer Pete stuck the paper in front of Mr. Pratt. "Did you sign this?"

Mr. Pratt looked at Mr. Fraley like he needed permission to speak. But Mr. Fraley was locked up against a slow-burning panic. "Yeah, I signed it," Mr. Pratt finally said. "Me and Bob Fraley sign all of 'em."

"Then you should know what this is about. Both of you are being arrested for falsifying state medical records."

All of the color drained from Mr. Pratt's face.

Mr. Fraley let out a nervous laugh. "You've got to be kidding," he said.

Officer Pete locked eyes on him again. "Does it appear I've developed a sense of humor? If I have, it would be news to a lot of people."

The quivering in Mr. Fraley's jowls traveled down into his hands until his entire body seemed on the verge of explosion. "Hypocrites!" he yelled. "You dump these dogs in my facility and you know damn well you don't wanna see any of them again! I make your life easy! I do the dirty work and you wanna come in here and throw this at my face! This is how you repay me! You know how it works!"

"Turn around. Put your hands behind your back."

"You want these criminals walking your sidewalks at night? Who's going to keep your kids safe?"

"I am," Officer Pete said. He grabbed Mr. Fraley by the shoulder and spun him and wrestled his wrists together. Officer Don grabbed Mr. Pratt and did the same.

"Bob?" Mr. Pratt said.

"Shut up!" Mr. Fraley replied. "Don't say anything else! I know Judge Mackin, you know!"

"Yeah, I know," Officer Pete said. "I talked to him this mornin'. He said he never did like you to begin with. Get 'em out of here, Don."

Two policemen jerked Mr. Pratt and Mr. Fraley away and led them out of the yard. Then Officer Pete turned to us. He scanned all the boys from one end of the fence to the other, taking deep breaths through his nose and swelling at the chest.

"Who's Paco?" he asked.

Paco lifted his hand.

"You need medical attention?"

"I'm okay," Paco said.

"Anybody else here need medical attention?"

No one said anything.

"Effective immediately, the entire staff of the Hellenweiler Boys' Home has been suspended pending investigation. The Tuscaloosa Police Department will be taking over the facility until we get to the bottom of the situation."

Then Officer Pete looked down at Jack. "Stand up," he said.

Jack got to his feet and stared at the policeman defiantly. "I didn't do anything."

"I've been haulin' you in and out of this place for two years. And you know what? You're slap out of leverage, son."

Jack didn't answer.

"That's right. As far as we know, you're on the only

195

report in the home that hasn't been tampered with. Says you assaulted a resident without provocation. Officer Crawley, take this boy to the station and get him in a real jail. Judge Mackin wants to try him as an adult."

"I want my lawyer," Jack said.

"Oh, you'll get him. We're gonna let you share a cell with him. Seems he's in a bit of trouble himself over blackmailin' a public official."

Jack swallowed and looked around like he might find someone to help him. But no one made a move.

"I want my dad!"

"He'll be there too. You'll be right at home."

A policeman walked up to Jack and grabbed him and took him away.

After Jack was gone, Officer Pete faced us again. "It's gonna take my people a while to get to the bottom of exactly what's been goin' on in here. Regardless of what we find, I imagine the entire staff will be replaced. Until that time, we go by my rules. And I'll tell you right now, violence of any sort will not be tolerated by me or any of my officers."

Officer Pete waved his hand in the air toward the building. "Now, I want everyone except Hal Mitchell to report to the mess hall. And I want you to sit at the tables in the order of your shirt numbers."

I turned to Paco, but he already knew what I was thinking.

"Find Caboose," he said.

I took a deep breath and nodded.

Paco and the boys stood and Officer Pete's policemen

escorted them out of the play yard. I turned to Mr. Wellington. "Where's Daddy?"

"He's out there waiting on you. You ready to go home?"

"I never been so ready to go anywhere in my life. Get me out of here."

38

Mr. Wellington and I stopped at the front office. It was quiet and empty of everyone except for Officer Pete. He was going through the filing cabinets, looking for more information about what had been happening at Hellenweiler. When Mr. Wellington asked about my jacket and release forms he shook his head and kept flipping through the files. He said he didn't know where everything was yet and didn't have time to worry about details. He'd bring by anything we needed later.

"Thanks, Officer Pete," I said.

He stopped what he was doing and looked over at me. "No problem, kid . . . I don't wanna see you again."

"Nossir," I said.

"Go on. Get outta here."

We walked out the front gate of Hellenweiler and the world opened up in front of me. I breathed deep and pulled in the faint smell of the pines over the asphalt parking lot. "Almost there, Paco," I said to myself.

I saw Daddy leaning against the truck, cleaning his fingernails with a pocketknife. He looked up and a stupid grin spread across his face. I ran to him and let him wrap his big arms around me.

"What took you so long?" I said.

He beat my back a couple of times with his fist. "You all right?"

"Yeah. Now I am."

Mr. Wellington caught up with us and waited patiently. After a while I pulled away and leaned against the tailgate and faced them.

"I just can't believe I'm really out of there," I said.

"It took some time to get the right people involved," Mr. Wellington replied. "It was quite an accusation. I imagine this might make national news. Judge Mackin threw out your conduct report and he'll probably throw out a bunch more before it's all over with."

"Long as Mr. Fraley does jail time, I'm good," I replied. "Stick him in solitary and see how *he* likes it."

"Well, that's not gonna be my call, Hal. My objective was to get you home again. Now that that's done, I'm really retired. So you better stay out of trouble," he joked.

We all shook hands and Mr. Wellington turned to go. I went around to the passenger side of the truck and got in. I sank into the seat and slammed the door. I breathed in the tobacco and diesel smell of it and rubbed my hand on the armrest. Daddy got in and cranked it.

"You don't know how bad I missed this old truck."

"Let's get you back and you can dog her out in the clay pit a little bit. How's that sound?"

"Sounds good. But I can't go home yet. As much as I want all this to be over, it's not."

"What are you talkin' about?"

"We gotta go to the junkyard. A friend of mine got out this mornin' and I think he's gonna be there. He's pretty messed up in his head. I gotta see him and let him know everything's okay. Make sure he don't do anything stupid."

* * *

It was dusk when we pulled off the blacktop before the junkyard. The smell of the pines came strong and thick as turpentine. I told Daddy to wait in the truck for me while I walked back to the house. Then I set out down the dirt road amid the cicadas thrumming in the night air. There was no moon out, but the stars were bright overhead. It had been a while since I'd seen a sky that wasn't flooded with fake city light. It felt healthy to the eyes.

The junk cars lay in darkness on either side of me like sleeping beasts in beds of overgrown field grass. I'd never been there at night, but I was more at home in that twenty-acre graveyard than just about anywhere. Back when I'd lived with Daddy I'd walked all the foot-pressed paths between their rusted-out hulks, searching their bowels for still-greased, shiny parts that would fix or improve our truck and equipment at the clay pit. It was the kind of place that made me feel like my life was right.

I came to the end of the road and saw the outline of the frame house to my left. I'd been inside it before. It was nothing more than a small front porch, one bedroom, a kitchen, and a bathroom. The windows were all broken out and the interior had been picked through and vandalized long before I'd first seen the place. A whip-poor-will called from deep inside the forest, but the building was dark and silent. Too silent. Somehow I knew he was in there.

"Caboose?" I said.

No answer.

I went closer to the house, careful to step around the junk parts lying in the grass. It seemed hundreds of mechanical projects had been started and abandoned in the front yard.

"Caboose?" I called again.

Still nothing. The whip-poor-will sounded once more. "You know, we ain't at Hellenweiler now."

I heard something move inside. The front door creaked open and I saw a big body silhouetted against the darkness. I froze as fear darted up my spine. "That better be you, Caboose."

He didn't move.

"You better say somethin' before I throw one of these car parts at you. Makin' me nervous up there like that."

"Maybe I'm seein' things," he said.

I let out my breath. "Man, what's wrong with you, you big spook? I said we'd do it, didn't I?"

No answer.

"You don't even have electricity out here?"

He stepped onto the porch and moved sideways. He sat in a creaky rocking chair against the wall. "We used to," he said.

I went up the steps and leaned against one of the columns across from him. "They busted that place wide open. Mr. Fraley's done."

He didn't respond.

"What you been doin' out here?" I asked him.

"Lookin' for things I remember."

"Like what?"

He studied me for a moment. "I had some baseball cards," he finally said. "And a rock polisher."

"You gotta be kiddin' me. People been breakin' the windows out of this place and stealin' from it for years."

"I got nothin'. I got nobody."

I stood up. "You got somebody. And you ain't stayin' here tonight. There's a bed at my place you can use until you get straight."

Caboose shook his head.

"You ain't findin' nothin' tonight, Caboose. You come stay at the clay pit until we get this place cleaned up. Daddy's waitin' on us."

I turned and stepped off the porch. "Come on," I said. "Let's get out of here."

Caboose stood slowly and followed. "I'll walk with you to the road," he said.

"The hell. We're done with all that state home business and everything before it. We got a clean jacket, Caboose. Got stars and trees and night sounds."

"Got nothin'."

"Keep walkin'. I ain't leavin' without you. Stupid rock polisher."

Caboose tailed me across the yard and we turned and started up the dirt road again. "I've been thinkin'. I could find enough parts in this place to make us a race car for the dirt track. And you could use it until I'm old enough for a license. What you think about that?"

Caboose didn't say anything.

"But that's long-term. Tomorrow we can go down to my uncle Tom's lake and stretch the trotline. And my girl-friend's got a big sister you might like to take out."

Caboose grunted.

"Serious, man. She's good-lookin' too. You saw her across that field."

"How's Paco?" he asked.

"He's fine. And he'll be a lot better when he knows you ain't gonna go off and do anything crazy."

"He was right about you," he said.

"Whatever. Between all his funny talk and your no talk, I can't believe we got anything done."

Daddy was surprised when I walked up with Caboose, but he's never been one to turn anybody out. I introduced him and they shook hands while Daddy's eyes sized him up.

"Caboose needs a place to stay," I said.

"Well, squeeze in here. We got room."

Caboose eyed me.

"Get in," I said.

39

Even though it was dark, I could tell something was different about the clay pit. As the house trailer came into view under the utility light, I saw that all of the old washing machines and refrigerators and broken cars had been hauled away.

"Place looks clean, Daddy."

"I told you about havin' the fidgets since I stopped drinkin'. I can hardly sit still."

"Where'd you put it all?"

"I dug a big hole out there with the front-end loader and buried it."

"Well, that's good."

"Wait'll you see what else," he said.

We pulled closer and our headlights lit up the yard. What used to be red clay mud was now a square of freshly mown lawn.

"You even planted some grass!"

Daddy spit out the window. "Well, you know."

Our two bloodhounds came running up the hill from the shop and leaped at the truck and bawled and scraped at the door with their toenails.

"Hey, Snapper!" I yelled. "Hey, Sawbone!"

We pulled to a stop and I nudged Caboose. "Come on, I'll show you around."

"They gonna bite me?"

"They ain't gonna bite. Go on."

After we got out, Daddy took the truck down to the shop where he had to put the front-end loader up. Caboose stood over me and watched while I rolled around with the dogs. After a minute I managed to stand and fend them off.

"Go on inside, Caboose! I'm gonna have to make a run for it!"

I watched him go into the trailer, then I started running for the shop. When the bloodhounds bolted past me, I spun around and made a dash for the trailer. It didn't take them but a second to figure they'd been faked out. I just made it inside before they crashed into the door, and I saw their faces bouncing up outside the window.

I showed Caboose my room. I had two mattresses on the floor and pointed out the one he could sleep on. "We'll throw you a new sheet on there. Nobody even uses it anymore except the dogs. Daddy'll make 'em stay outside again now that I'm back. I'll be sleepin' right there next to you."

"I'll be fine," Caboose said.

"Come on. I'll take you down the hill and show you the shop."

"I think I'll just lay here and go to sleep," he said.

"You sure? We haven't even eaten."

"I'm sure. I'm tired, Hal. You go ahead."

"All right. But you ain't takin' your shoes off in there. I'll go get a roller pan and put some gasoline in it and put it outside the front door. You soak your feet in that and it'll get 'em all good."

"Thanks, Hal."

"No problem. You can use that blanket and sheet off my bed too. I'll get another one in a little while."

"Okay."

"Don't you go runnin' off either. I'm gonna be lookin' up here."

That night Daddy and I cooked hamburgers and talked late into the night while Caboose slept.

"Your boss gonna get onto you about skippin' out today?" I asked him.

"He better not. I been puttin' in eighty-hour weeks. You wait'll you see those trucks lined up tomorrow."

"When's he gonna get you some help?"

"I hope soon."

"What about Caboose?" I said.

"You think he can run a loader?"

"You can teach him if he don't."

"I need somebody I can count on," Daddy said.

"So does he."

The next morning I woke to the sound of dump trucks groaning and putting on their air brakes outside. I turned over and saw Caboose with his eyes open. "Feels good to wake up outside the fence, don't it?" I said.

Caboose nodded.

"Daddy won't need the truck today. You wanna go fishin'?"

"I've got stuff to do."

"You ain't gotta do nothin'. We'll go out to Uncle Tom's lake and catch some bream. Then you can drive me to Carla's school so I can see her."

Caboose studied his feet.

"They smell better now, don't they?"

"They smell like gas and they burn and itch."

"That's good. Killin' all that stuff."

Caboose drove us into town. We bought sandwich meat, bread, and worms at the gas station and then headed for Uncle Tom's lake.

"What you think about my truck?"

"It drives good."

"It'll get a gear, won't it?"

"It's a good truck."

"All the pieces I got out of your salvage yard, so you prob'ly own half of it."

Caboose looked sideways at me.

"Well, nobody was there," I said.

I waited for him to smile, but he didn't.

"Come on, now. I know you feel better today. What are you thinkin' about?"

"How long it's gonna take to clean up that house. I got a lot to do. Maybe I don't need to go fishin'."

"What if you let Daddy teach you how to drive the loader? Bet you could scrape that yard clean in about five minutes. Push all that stuff out your front door, dig a hole, and bury it."

Caboose frowned.

"You know I talked to him about givin' you a job at the clay pit. He needs somebody else."

"What'd he say?"

"Said he'd think about it. I'll bet if you told him you were interested, he'd get you saddled up."

"I don't know," he said.

* * *

The lake was just as I remembered it. Except for the cypress trees being a little bigger, it hadn't changed a bit. We spent the day bream fishing and napping in the shade. For once I was glad that Caboose didn't say much. I didn't have anything on my mind but Carla and fishing, and that's all I wanted for a while.

"You were right," Caboose said. "It wasn't a coin toss."

"Forget it, man. We're not talkin' about that place."

"He beat me at arm wrestling."

I turned to him. His eyes were still closed. "Hah! He out-muscled you!"

Caboose frowned.

"I can't wait to ask him about that."

"I don't mind tellin' you now. It doesn't matter anymore. I don't care what they think about me."

I didn't say anything. Caboose opened his eyes and stared at the treetops. I turned away and studied my cork.

"You don't have to be the same out here," I said. "All that stuff behind us was just a bunch of things gone wrong."

We didn't say anything for a while.

Finally Caboose said, "I'm not as mad about it all as I was."

"You got other things to think about now. There wasn't anything to do at Hellenweiler but be mad."

"I know what you're tryin' to do, Hal."

"Then you tell me what I wanna hear."

"I don't know if I can forget what they did to Marty."

"I never asked you to forget. But you think about bein' out here in a place like this the rest of your life while Mr.

Fraley and the rest of those guards sit in a jail cell. That's punishment, right there. And you did it to 'em. It don't get any better than that. You let 'em sit in that prison and think about it."

"I never thought of it that way."

"I didn't either until just then."

Caboose sat up and stared over the lake. "I think I'm gonna be okay," he said.

"Damn right you are."

Daddy had a little stick-up clock on the dash of the truck and it showed two-thirty when we started for Gainesville. Rhonda and Carla would be out of school in a half hour. I slid down in my seat and put my feet on the dash.

"I hope we can find 'em," I said.

Caboose didn't answer me.

"I don't wanna have to go to her house yet. Her daddy's gonna wanna give me one of those talks. I hate that."

"We'll find her," Caboose said.

We drove into the student parking lot five minutes before school let out. Caboose downshifted and drove slow while I searched for Rhonda's car. All of the other cars and trucks looked new and shiny compared to what we were in.

"This is another world, ain't it?" I said.

"What kind of car is it?"

"Red Grand Am. The one that drove in the field that day . . . Where do these people get money for cars like this?"

Caboose didn't answer me.

"It's been so long since I've been to a real school . . ."

I continued to scan the cars. Then I saw the Grand Am ahead of us. "Pull off right here," I said. "I'll walk over."

He looked at me.

"I know. I just feel like a redneck in this thing."

Caboose parked the truck and I got out. The school bell sounded before I'd made it to Rhonda's car. I jammed my hands into my pockets and sucked up against the jitters in my stomach. Seconds later the kids poured out of the building and came toward us. I got to the Grand Am and leaned against the trunk.

As the kids came closer, I noticed how clean and neat they all looked. How colorful they were, dressed in the latest fashions, everyone unique and independent. All of the girls looked so fresh and the boys so sure of themselves. I suddenly had doubts and pulled my hands out of my pockets and stood up straight. *What am I doin' here?* I mumbled to myself. I looked toward the truck and Caboose was walking my way. He stopped beside me and I looked at him and met his eyes. He didn't have to say anything. Just the look was all I needed. I turned and faced the students again and there was Carla. To me she looked like the prettiest of them all. And she was my girl and I was going to make her proud of me. A second later she saw me and a smile spread across her face. She ran to me and hugged me and I squeezed her hard and breathed in the smell of her hair.

Dear Paco,
    I'm home again. The pine trees are waiting for you out here and Caboose is going to be fine. He's

started working with my daddy if you can believe that. We're gonna get a second front-end loader and he'll drive it full time. He's also got a little house we've been fixing. It might be ready for the two of you to live in by the time you get out. You better come see us right after you walk through those gates. It all gets better again, I promise. See you soon.

Your friend,
Hal

Discussion Questions

1. Do you think Hal deserves to be at the Hellenweiler Boys' Home? Why?

2. Do you agree with Hal's choice to stay unassociated with the Ministers and the Hounds? Is this a good decision? Why? If you were Hal, would you make the same decision?

3. Who do you think is a better leader, Paco or Jack? Who do you think is stronger? Why?

4. Why do both gangs leave Caboose alone? Why does Caboose never say anything?

5. How did Hal's experiences with Moon Blake change Hal's personality?

6. Why do the boys at Hellenweiler lie about how they got there?

7. Why did Paco take a beating from Jack? What was he trying to achieve?

8. How was Paco different before he came to Hellenwei-ler? Why did he change?

9. Have you ever gotten in trouble with the law? Did the experience change you?

10. Did you like the ending of the book? Do you think that Caboose will still seek revenge from the guards?

GOFISH

WATT KEY

© Ward Faulk

When did you realize you wanted to be a writer?

I wrote my first story when I was ten. It was about a collie surviving a tornado. I was into Jim Kjelgaard, a writer of dog books, then, and I wanted to try and make stories like his. I kept writing short stories for fun throughout the rest of my prep school days. My high school creative writing teacher convinced me that I had talent as an author and this gave me the idea that maybe I was meant to be a writer. It wasn't until my sophomore year in college that I knew this for certain. I was running the outdoor skills department at a boys' camp in Texas. I was alone and far away from home, with lots of free time in a little cabin by the Guadalupe River. I wrote my first novel there. Although it was a terrible book that will never be published, it was the most satisfying thing I'd ever done. After that summer, I continued to write a novel a year without regard to whether it would be published or not. I'd written ten novels by the time *Alabama Moon* sold.

What was your worst subject in school?

I remember making an 88 out of 100 on just about every test I took in high school, regardless of the subject. So I wasn't an outstanding student, but neither was I a poor one. At my school, 88 was about average. Before I went to college, my parents took me to see a psychologist in New Orleans. I went through a series of aptitude tests that were supposed to help us decide what profession I was best suited for. Basically, I scored an 88 on everything. The conclusion was that I would always have a hard time deciding what I wanted to be because none of my abilities seemed to stand out above the rest. This didn't help me directly, but ever since then, I've been conscious of the fact that I need to specialize in one thing to be outstanding at anything. For example, as much as I would like to play a musical instrument, I don't. I shun it like a bad vice. I know I would enjoy it too much and it would take away from my focus on being the best writer I can be.

What was your first job?
My brothers and sisters and I always had chores assigned to us that we didn't get paid for. My first duties were emptying the wastebaskets around the house, feeding various pets (we had lots of animals), and raking and mowing the lawn. I landed my first paying job when I was about eight years old. I was the fly killer for the snack bar at a resort not far from my home. I killed them with a washcloth, stored them in a paper cup, and received ten cents per fly. As soon as I would get enough dimes, I would cash in my pay for a drink to quench my thirst.

How did you celebrate publishing your first book?
My wife and I went to the Mexican restaurant up the street. It was a fairly low-key celebration. It took a while for me to accept that I'd gotten a legitimate book deal. You may have seen the episode of *The Waltons* when John-Boy gets scammed by the vanity publisher. He told all of his friends and family that he'd gotten a book deal and they had a big celebration for him. Then he got a letter from the publisher

asking him how many of his books he wanted to pay them to print. It was a scam. This exact thing happened to me years before I sold *Alabama Moon* and it was very embarrassing and eye-opening.

Where do you write your books?
After college, I built a small camp several miles into the swamp that you can only get to by boat. I made it from lumber that washed up on the beach after a hurricane. It took me nearly every weekend for a year to complete it. I develop and outline most of my ideas up there. The bulk of my actual writing is done at home in a spare bedroom that doubles as my study.

Where do you find inspiration for your writing?
I'm not always inspired to write. Fortunately, I have a backlog of stories in my head that I feel have to be written whether I'm in the mood for it or not. I often tell people that writing is like an addiction to me. I liken this addiction to people who jog every day. I don't feel good about myself unless I'm doing it. Most of the time, it's a very enjoyable process. Sometimes, it's not. But I decided long ago that I was supposed to be a writer, so that's what I do.

When you finish a book, who reads it first?
My wife, Katie, reads my first drafts most of the time. I've learned that if I don't want her to read it, it's probably not ready. Then my agent reads it, and finally my editor.

Are you a morning person or a night owl?
I'm a night owl. But to feel good and productive, I have to have eight hours of sleep, no more, no less. I usually write from about eight until eleven at night and get up at seven in the morning.

What's your idea of the best meal ever?
Rib eye steak. Egg noodles with real butter and garlic. Real mashed potatoes without gravy. Cream cheese spinach. Brewed iced tea with lemon, real sugar, and mint. Lemon pie without the meringue for dessert.

Where do you go for peace and quiet?
My swamp camp

What makes you laugh out loud?
Mark Twain

What do you value most in your friends?
Honesty. Originality.

What is your favorite TV show?
I don't recommend television. One day I was driving through Mississippi and came across a folk artist with a yard full of his scrap iron creations. Out front was a sign that read "Look what I did while you were watching TV." I like his attitude.

What's the best advice you have ever received about writing?
Continue to write even when you don't feel like it. If you're a real writer, that's what you have to do. I knew this on an instinctive level for many years, but never heard it described as well as what a painter friend of mine told me. I was watching him create an oil painting of an outdoor scene. He was doing his work in a small, rocking boat, crouched beneath an umbrella in the pouring rain. I remarked that he was the most dedicated artist I'd ever met. He responded by telling me that he wasn't an artist, he was a professional painter.

The government is the enemy. Or so Moon's father said before his death. Now Moon must follow his father's last request to seek others like him in Alaska.

But once he's alone, Moon becomes the property of the government he had avoided all his life, caught in a world he does not understand.

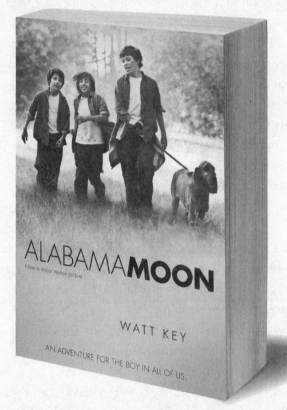

Follow Moon's journey north in
ALABAMA **MOON**
by Watt Key.

It seemed like everything started going wrong the summer before Pap's accident. We heard through Mr. Abroscotto, who owned the general store in Gainesville, that International Paper Company had run into hard times and was selling off some of its land. Pap said that the paper company had owned the forest as long as we'd been there and that they were too big to know about us. If they sold out to smaller landowners, we'd likely be found.

I could tell that Pap was worried. He told me that the swimming hole was off limits and that I was to stay close to the shelter unless I was checking traps or getting drinking water. Without the creek to swim in, the days were hotter than any I can remember. We spent afternoons sitting in the shelter, covered with the tannic acid from boiled acorns to keep off the ticks and mosquitoes. Pap had me practice my reading while he carved fish hooks from briars and bound sticks to make catfish traps.

It wasn't two weeks after our visit to Mr. Abroscotto's store that surveyors found our shelter while we were out checking the traps. When Pap and I returned, we saw their orange vests through the trees and we ducked into the bushes and watched them as they walked around the shelter. They stayed there for about an hour, poking at our things. I asked Pap if they were the government, and he said no, but they weren't much better.

"Should we shoot at 'em?"

"No."

"If they're not any better than—"

"When the war comes, you'll know."

"How?"

"I'll tell you."

The next morning, Pap woke me at daybreak. "Get up," he said. "We need to go into town and find out what's happenin'."

I got excited about going to Mr. Abroscotto's. It was the only time I saw any of the outside world. But I was careful not to let Pap know how I felt. He said showing ourselves to outsiders was the most dangerous part of how we lived. One slipup and the law would be all over us. A trip to the store wasn't anything he wanted to see me excited over.

"We gonna take somethin' to sell, Pap?"

"Ain't got time. Get your britches on."

As the sun slipped over the trees, we made the six-mile trip to Mr. Abroscotto's. We used to sell our furs to him, but it had been more than three years since we'd sold any. He said the prices were so low that he lost money just paying for gasoline to get them to Birmingham, where he sold them to companies that made clothes and things out of them. Since then, we had sold him the meat instead, along with vegetables we grew in the garden, and we bought what we wanted of the outside world with the money he gave us.

Most of the journey was through the forest, but the last half mile was on the road to avoid the big swamp. Pap said this was okay because the road was straight and long and we could hear cars coming in either direction before they saw us. We had time to slip down into the ditch and lie still until they passed.

The store was on the outskirts of town, and the only building nearby was a small brick one that Pap said was owned by the power company. We could see a traffic light another half mile up the road which Pap said was the only one in Gainesville. I liked to watch the light as long as I could before Pap hurried me past the gas pumps and into the store. I'd seen a tractor go under the light once and even a yellow school bus.

Mr. Abroscotto was a strong man for somebody his age, like he used to be a logger or a policeman. His skin was dark as leather and his snow-white hair stood out against it. This time he told us that a lawyer named Mr. Wellington had purchased eleven thousand acres from the paper company. The property went from the Noxubee River to the big swamp and from the highway to Major's Creek on the east and west sides. By Mr. Abroscotto's landmarks, I figured our shelter was just about in the middle of Mr. Wellington's property. Pap must have been thinking the same thing. He walked out of the store without even saying goodbye. I hurried after him and had to walk fast to keep up.

"Slow down, Pap."

He didn't answer me.

"Pap?"

He turned quickly and grabbed my arm and jerked me along beside him. "You keep up this time," he said. "Run if you have to."

A couple of weeks passed before heavy equipment started making a road and a clearing three miles away. Pap was nervous all the time and snapped at me when I made the smallest mistake. He got particular about me stepping on sticks and making noise when we walked through the forest. He kept stopping and touching my shoulder, which meant for me to be still and listen. I could tell by the way he acted that all those workers and equipment meant trouble.

We began to check our catfish traps at night, slipping down the banks of the Noxubee River by moonlight. In the mornings we remained close to the shelter unless we had something special to do. We worked the garden, tending our cucumbers, eggplant, and beets. All of those vegetables, when spaced the right way, grew hidden among the natural forest plants and wouldn't give us away if someone was to come across them. In the heat of the day, we'd get back into the shelter again and stay there until late afternoon. Pap began to watch and listen out the window slits as much as he worked on things. Even my reading began to make him nervous.

"Read to yourself, boy. You're too old to read out loud anymore."

A month later, Pap and I were traveling a trail to the southeast of the shelter to get some red clay for pot making. We were less than a mile from the new clearing when Pap suddenly held his hand up in the air. I knew the signal and stopped. We stood there for several seconds and then, through the whine of mosquitoes, I heard hammering.

"Somebody's makin' somethin', Pap?"

I saw him clench his teeth and narrow his eyes. "Shhh!" he said.

After a few more seconds, Pap continued down the trail.

"What is it, Pap?"

"House."

"Somebody gonna live there?"

"Yeah."

I could tell Pap didn't want to talk about it, so I followed behind him and didn't ask any more questions.

After we heard the hammering, Pap couldn't keep his mind on his chores. He'd get me to working on something at the shelter and he'd say he had to walk off in the woods and tend to things. He was usually gone for a couple of hours. He didn't want me to know where he went, but I knew it was to watch the hammering.

One day he said, "You finish scalin' those fish. I got to go look for somethin' I left down the trail."

"I wanna go, Pap."

"Just a one-man job."

"I've only got two fish left."

Pap stared off at the treetops and bit his bottom lip. "All right," he finally said. "Come on, then."

Pap never meant to look for anything. We slipped through the forest using gallberry and cane for cover until we got to where the house was being built. They had cemented concrete blocks together and run timbers across them for the floor supports. The yard was stacked with lumber for the rest of the framing. I turned to Pap, waiting for him to tell me what it meant. His face was worried pale.

"Gonna be a big house, Pap?" I finally asked.

"Big huntin' lodge," he mumbled.

"I've never seen somethin' built that big."

He nodded his head and motioned for us to head back to the shelter.

We didn't go to the lodge together again. The days began to grow cooler and the breezes told us that fall was arriving. Things had changed between Pap and me. Even though I was with him just about every minute of the day, I didn't feel like he knew I was there. He was far away in thought most of the time, and even though I watched his face, I couldn't get clues to what he was thinking.

We got the steel traps out of storage and oiled them and wired the parts that were broken. The maple leaves had just started to turn and I knew we were over a month away from trapping season. But Pap didn't seem to be doing things in the right order anymore. One day he told me to go gather mulberries. It had been five months since the last mulberry dropped.

"Pap, there's not any mulberries."

"Just do what I tell you," he said.

I waited for a few seconds to see if he would realize his mistake, but he went back to sharpening his knife. I didn't know what to do, so I stepped into the forest and started walking, thinking that if I stayed gone long enough it would convince him that I'd tried my best.

Once I got away from the shelter, it felt good to be on my own again after such a long time staying close to Pap and feeling his worries. I looked up into the trees and studied the yellows and reds of the changing leaves. The birds flitted about and made shrill cries from deep in the bush. It felt like I could breathe easier, and the smells of cedar and stinkbugs flowed into my nose.

Without meaning to, I wandered within hearing distance of the lodge. Once the sound of power tools and hammers reached my ears, I was too curious not to slip closer for a better look.

The workmen had moved a house trailer onto the site, and they seemed to be living in it. More lumber was stacked in the yard, along with roofing material and bricks. The lodge was already framed two stories high. I wanted to stay and watch the men working, but Pap's warnings about contact with outsiders started to play in my head. I crept back into the forest and took a different trail to the shelter.

Pap was sitting outside, weaving a basket from muscadine vine when I walked up. I stood in front of him, ready to tell him why I didn't have any mulberries, but he didn't ask about them or anything else.

Finally I said, "They're puttin' walls on that lodge, Pap."

His fingers stopped and he looked up at me. "I don't ever want you goin' near it again."

"But it's not even finished."

"I don't care. You heard what I said."

"You think maybe when the lawyer moves in we could talk to him and he'd let us stay on?"

Pap looked at me again. "I don't know, son! Why don't you get back to work and forget about that lawyer and his business."

———

As fall passed, the leaves began dropping from the trees and the forest canopy became a solid green fan of pine needles. We pulled our deerskin jackets from between the cedar boards and waterproofed them with mink oil for the season. The carrots would stay in the ground for a while longer, but the other garden vegetables needed to come out before the first frost. I was always excited about the last harvest of the year because I knew it meant we'd go to Mr. Abroscotto's store to sell whatever we had.

I was afraid that Pap might tell me to stay behind, but he didn't. He shouldered the sack of vegetables one morning and told me to get my jacket and come with him. Pap would usually be walking slow and studying the forest. He'd look for deer scrapes and hog rootings and any other signs that might help us find game once the weather turned cold. But that day his mind was on other things and he stared straight ahead and didn't slow down.

Mr. Abroscotto was sitting behind the counter reading a newspaper when we walked in.

"Mornin', George," Pap said.

Mr. Abroscotto set down his paper and stood up. "Mornin', Oli. How you, Moon?"

"I'm fine," I said.

"What do you two have for me?"

Pap showed Mr. Abroscotto the sack of vegetables. "Cucumbers, eggplant, and beets," he said.

Mr. Abroscotto took the sack to the scales. He weighed the vegetables separately and then put them all in a brown box on the floor.

"How does twenty bucks sound?" he said.

"If that's what you can do, I don't guess we've got much choice."

Mr. Abroscotto nodded and paid him from the register. Pap fidgeted the money into his pocket, and I knew he was in a better mood.

"What more have you heard about that lawyer?" Pap asked.

Mr. Abroscotto shook his head. "Haven't heard much. See his workmen in here all the time."

"You know when they're gonna be done?"

"They're tellin' me December. Gonna be moved in for Christmas."

I stood behind Pap and looked around the store at the shelves of candy and canned food. I was careful not to let Pap see me, because I knew it would make him snap at me. Sometimes he made me wait outside while he went in and traded. He said it was too tempting for a boy inside the store.

"What's he gonna do with that big place?" Pap asked.

"I hear he likes to squirrel hunt."

Pap shook his head and looked mad. "All that to hunt squirrels?"

"Guess some people got more money than they know what to do with."

"Guess so," Pap grumbled. "Let me have some salt, some .22 bullets, vinegar, box of nails, and matches."

Mr. Abroscotto left to collect our supplies.

"How about some sugar this time, Pap?"

"Don't need sugar."

"How about some canned peas like we had that one time?"

"We've got a pile of toasted acorns you haven't touched yet."

I figured he wasn't in the mood to buy extras. "We've got everything we need already, don't we, Pap?"

Pap nodded. "Got everything we need," he repeated.

We walked back up the road and into the forest, where we took a trail that I liked through a grove of cedars and tall field grass. That was the last time Pap left the forest.